W9-AEE-608

A MOTHER FOR HIS TWINS

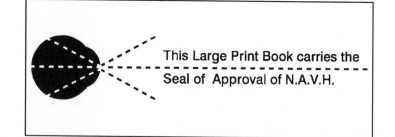

This Large Print Book carries the
Seal of Approval of N.A.V.H.

A MOTHER FOR HIS TWINS

LUCY CLARK

THORNDIKE PRESS
A part of Gale, Cengage Learning

GALE
CENGAGE Learning™

Detroit • New York • San Francisco • New Haven, Conn • Waterville, Maine • London

LIBRARY OF CONGRESS CATALOGING-IN-PUBLICATION DATA

Clark, Lucy.
   A mother for his twins / by Lucy Clark. — Large print ed.
      p. cm. — (Thorndike Press large print clean reads)
   ISBN-13: 978-1-4104-2466-2 (alk. paper)
   ISBN-10: 1-4104-2466-9 (alk. paper)
   1. Twins—Fiction. 2. Widowers—Fiction. 3. Surgeons—Fiction.
4. Large type books. I. Title.
PR9619.4.C53M68 2010
823'.92—dc22   2009047185

Published in 2010 by arrangement with Harlequin Books S.A.

Printed in the United States of America
1 2 3 4 5 6 7 14 13 12 11 10

Dear Reader,

When writing *A Mother for His Twins,* we knew we wanted to include the most adorable little girls, so innocent and lovable, just waiting for the right person to come along and be their new mommy.

Both Jennifer and Jasper meet in the lovely suburb of Parramatta. Each have experienced such heartache and pain in their pasts, but where Jasper had managed to move on, through the love of his girls, Jennifer was still trapped by the hurt. It was not only Jasper who was able to help Jen put her troubles to rest but also his sweet girls, Lilly and Lola. (Incidentally, our daughter chose the names for the girls!)

Setting the book in Parramatta was an easy choice. It's an area that isn't as busy as Sydney. Although there's a lot of hustle and bustle, there is also the opportunity for delightful walks along the banks of the Parramatta River and catamaran rides into Sydney Harbour.

We hope you enjoy *A Mother for His Twins* and fall in love with those delightful little girls just as much as Jennifer and Jasper.

Warmest regards,
Lucy Clark

To DT — my Scottish muse.

Psalms 34:17

PROLOGUE

'I'll get it. I'll get it!' Four-year-old Lola called as she raced towards the ringing phone.

'No. I'll get it. I'll get it,' Lilly contradicted, her little legs working as fast as they could to catch up to her twin.

'Girls. Please. Settle down. Jen, can you get the phone, please?' Sara begged, her hands all sticky with the bread dough she was kneading.

'Sure.' Jennifer shifted on the stool and reached for the phone receiver, which was situated on a high shelf specifically to prevent children answering it. 'Hello,' she said, the twins starting to whine and stamp their feet.

'I wanted to answer it.' Lilly wasn't happy. 'Daddy lets us answer the phone at home.'

'It was my turn,' Lola told her sister.

'Girls. Shh. Jen won't be able to hear.'

Jennifer smiled into the receiver as she

watched the two girls put their noses in their air, cross their arms over their chests and stomp back to the room they'd been playing in. 'Hello?' she repeated and listened carefully. The line was crackling with static and for a moment she wondered whether it was a crank call or yet another telemarketer. 'Hello?' She tried again and this time heard a faint male voice.

'Sara. Can you hear me? The line is bad.'

'It's not Sara.' Jennifer raised her voice slightly. 'Can I take a message?'

'Sara? I still can't hear you too well. Anyway, I just wanted to let you know I'm going to be later than usual. I've got to get things ready for the new boss coming in on Monday. Can you take the girls to my house at five o'clock?'

'I still can't hear you all that well. Did you say take the girls to your house at five?'

'Yes.'

Jennifer looked at Sara, who nodded. 'OK. That's fine.'

'Thanks. Gotta go.'

'OK. Bye.' But her words fell on deaf ears because he'd already hung up.

'Jasper's obviously been caught at work,' Sara stated matter-of-factly. 'He works too hard.'

Jennifer settled herself on the seat again

and watched her high-school friend turn a lump of dough into bread rolls. 'So run through it with me again. How exactly is Jasper related to you again?'

'Very loosely, but family is family as far as I'm concerned.'

'I'm not criticising,' Jennifer was quick to state. 'You know how I feel about family, especially when my own home life was ridiculously lonely.'

'You mean your parents having no time but for themselves and their careers? I do. Anyway, the link is that Jasper's wife was Matt's brother-in-law's sister.'

'Right.' Jennifer tried to figure it out. Matt was Sara's husband. They'd been married for the last ten years and had two boys who would be home from school very soon. 'So Matt's sister, Abby, is married to Don, and Jasper's wife was Don's sister?'

'Very good, Dr Thorngate. I can see all those years at university have served you well.'

Jennifer smiled. 'A very loose connection, but as you've said, family is family.' Jennifer sipped at her cup of tea, her tone more solemn. 'When did Jasper's wife die?'

'Three years ago. The twins had just turned one.'

She let out a slow breath. 'That would

have been so hard on him. A single parent to two very big handfuls.'

'Yes. They're gorgeous girls but totally full on all the time. It's always go, go, go with them.' Sara put the rolls onto a tray and put them in the oven to rise. 'Jasper had good support, though. He's close to his parents and his sister.'

'Good support,' Jennifer repeated softly, wishing she'd had more support when her own world had come crashing down eight years ago. Of course, Sara had been there for her, but Sara had been in a different part of the country and there had only been so much she could do. Now, though, Jennifer had come home. Back to Parramatta, an outer suburb of Sydney in New South Wales. Back to her old stomping ground. Back to where she'd first met Sara at school, back to where she'd originally gone to medical school and where she'd met Arturo. Next week, she'd be going back to the hospital where she'd studied as a medical student but now she'd be the head of the orthopaedic and trauma unit. It was a position she'd been striving for for far too long but finally, with a lot of hard work, commitment and sacrifice, she was making her dream come true. She just wished Arturo could have been there to witness it.

'Yes, poor Jasper took it very hard when Elisha died. Ovarian cancer.'

'Cancer in someone so young is never easy to deal with.' Jennifer's tone was quiet yet even she could hear the pain in her own voice. It didn't seem like eight years since Arturo had died, also of cancer, but it was, and still Jennifer felt the pain of his loss every single day. Thankfully, though, she had a very high-powered job and it was work that had kept her going. Work and Sara's continuing friendship, which meant the world to her.

'Anyway . . .' Jennifer shook her head and pasted on a bright smile. 'The girls are lovely and Jasper should be really proud of himself.'

Sara agreed. 'I think he is. He knows how lucky he is.'

'Where does he work?'

Sara stared at her for a moment, then quickly said, 'Oh, no. I didn't turn the oven on.' She brushed the flour from her hands and quickly turned the oven on low. 'The twins are so distracting sometimes. Absolutely gorgeous but distracting.' She returned her attention to cleaning up her kitchen. 'Looking forward to starting your new job on Monday?'

Jennifer shrugged, a little curious as to

why Sara hadn't answered her question. What was it about Jasper that was so secret? Was he a spy? Was he in the armed forces? Perhaps that was the case and given that Jennifer's own parents had been military personnel, moving around for most of her younger life, Sara hadn't wanted to mention it in case it upset her. She pushed the thoughts away. It didn't really matter and Sara was obviously waiting for an answer to her question. 'Yes and no.'

'That doesn't sound too good.'

'It's just apprehension and nerves. New hospital. New staff. New department.'

'Which you're in charge of. I thought you would have been happy to go back to your old hospital.'

'I am. Sort of. I just really want to do well as head of department. I've been working towards it for so long.'

'You'll settle in fast enough. Make some new friends. You'll be fine.'

'I don't think so.'

'Let me guess. The boss doesn't make friends easily?'

'*I* don't make friends easily,' Jennifer retorted. 'Being the boss just gives me that extra edge where people leave me alone.'

Sara washed her hands then turned to look at her friend. 'Is that what you really want? To come back to Parramatta and not make any new friends? To have everyone leave you alone like a princess locked in a tower?'

Jennifer shrugged and sighed. Was it? She'd told herself that this move back to Parramatta where she would start the job she'd been working towards for the past eight years was a fresh start. The problem was, she wasn't quite sure *how* fresh starts worked.

CHAPTER ONE

Jasper Edwards quickly packed his briefcase with a huge pile of papers, glad the amount would be drastically decreased after today. It was almost six-thirty in the morning and he needed to be leaving soon. He'd been up for at least an hour because Lola had been sneezing and coughing during the night. With the weather being so cold, it wasn't uncommon. The problem was that when one child got sick, the other usually followed suit. He made a mental note to watch Lilly for the first signs of the cold during the next few days.

'Feeling better, buttercup?' he asked as he brushed a hand over her blonde ringlets and kissed her cheek, glad her eyes didn't look so glassy this morning. At her nod, he scooped her up. 'Come on. Let's go wake Grandma and Grandpa. Daddy's got to be at the hospital early this morning.'

'Why?' Lola asked.

17

'Because the new boss is starting today.'

'Why?' Lilly chimed in, holding out her hands for her father to pick her up as well.

'Because she is.' Jasper balanced them.

'Why?' Lola asked.

'Because Daddy didn't want the job.'

'Why?' It was Lilly's turn again and Jasper couldn't keep his lips from twitching at their tag-team act.

'Because Daddy wants to spend more time with his gorgeous girls, that's why.'

'Why?' both of them asked together.

'Because Daddy loves you both.' He tickled their tummies and was rewarded with giggles from both, followed by coughing from Lola. They wrapped their arms about his neck and held on as he carried them through the ground floor of his house.

'Be the giant, Daddy. Be the giant,' Lilly demanded.

'Yeah. I love the giant,' Lola agreed.

'I love him, too,' Lilly added.

Knowing it would speed things up to acquiesce rather than argue, Jasper hunched his shoulders a little, maintaining his firm hold on each child. 'Grrroooowwwlll. I'm the great big giant from the land of Giganticor.' Jasper's voice was deeper than usual, making both girls giggle again, their arms tightening with excitement about his

18

neck as he crashed his way noisily up the stairs. 'I'm here to give yummy little girls a ride to the land of Grandparents. Are you both comfortable?'

'Yes,' they said in unison, their voices radiating utter glee.

'Grrrooooowwwlll. Off we go, then.' Walking with big steps and swaying from side to side, Jasper carefully made his way upstairs to his mother's kitchen. The house was the perfect arrangement for all concerned. He and the girls lived on the lower level and his parents lived upstairs. They had their own bedrooms, bathrooms, kitchen and living areas, giving privacy where privacy was needed and security for the girls when Jasper was called to the hospital in the middle of the night. They communicated via an intercom so if he was called out, he could buzz through to his parents and they knew to check on the girls, who had a child monitor situated in their perfectly pink bedroom.

His mother was in the kitchen, making coffee, as he crashed towards her, still growling. 'The granddaughter express from the land of Giganticor is here,' he announced, and Iris, his mother, came over and took the girls from him, one at a time.

'Oh, thank you, Mr Giant. You are so kind to deliver such beautiful girls to me.' When the girls were seated at the kitchen table, Jasper kissed his mother's cheek then poured himself a cup of coffee.

'Mmm. Just what the doctor ordered.'

Both girls giggled. 'You say that every morning, Daddy.' Lilly grinned up at him. 'Can I have some coffee?'

'I want some too,' Lola added.

'Ah. I believe Grandma has some yummy milk for you to have.'

'I want the coffee one.'

'I want it, too.'

Iris rolled her eyes. 'And you say *that* every morning,' she told her granddaughters. 'Kiss Daddy goodbye or he'll be late for work.'

Both girls puckered up and Jasper spent the next five minutes being smothered in kisses. 'I think I need another shower,' he remarked as he took the lunchbox Iris handed him.

'Make sure you eat that breakfast muffin sooner rather than later, Jasper Edwards, or there'll be trouble,' his mother warned.

'Yes, Mum,' he replied with mock meekness, then winked at his daughters. 'See you all tonight. Love you,' he called as he headed back down the stairs.

'Love you, too, Daddy,' the girls yelled, loud enough to wake up their grandpa, which only made Jasper smile even more.

■ ■ ■ ■

Jennifer walked through the hospital just before eight o'clock, eager to start work. The past week she'd spent at Sara's, trying to finding a suitable apartment, had been busy but very much the calm before the storm. The problem was, she hadn't found an apartment near the hospital and most of her belongings were still in Melbourne. If she didn't find a place soon, she'd have to put everything into storage and that was the last thing she wanted to do.

Anyway, she reminded herself, she would be spending most of her time here at the hospital, keeping busy. Work, work, work. She'd been thinking for some time that she needed to find a life outside work, but she was beginning to wonder if she ever would. Her one and only opportunity to have it all — to be a doctor, a wife and a mother — had been cruelly taken away from her when Arturo had died. Now that she'd achieved what she'd wanted to achieve professionally, she was beginning to realise how monocular her world was. For the past eight years she'd lived and breathed work, and it had been fine for the first few years. After that she'd simply fallen into a bad routine

where she'd spent more hours than necessary at the hospital, too many hours studying for her doctorate and declining every
social invitation that came her way.

In fact, for the past two years she'd barely
received any social invitations, and while
she tried not to let that bother her, telling
herself it was just as well because she'd have
had to turn them down anyway, quietly she
was upset at the way her life was turning
out. She knew Arturo wouldn't be happy
for her to be all alone and it was for that
reason alone that she'd jumped at the
chance to move back home to Parramatta.
Here, at least, she had the hope of finding
more depth to her life, mainly because when
she reflected on her past, Parramatta was
the one place she could remember being
truly happy.

On the drive to the hospital that morning,
she'd passed the high school she'd attended
with Sara. She'd passed the medical school
where she'd met Arturo on her first day.
She'd passed the gardens where Arturo had
kissed her for the first time, and she'd
passed the small hospital chapel where his
memorial service had been held.

The hospital itself had changed a great
deal since she'd been a lowly medical
student but she was able to navigate her way

to the orthopaedic department where her new office was situated. She walked up to the reception desk and was met by a smiling woman she guessed to be in her fifties.

'Dr Thorngate?'

'Yes.'

'Welcome. I'm Martha. Come through. Dr Edwards — he's been acting head of department — is in your office ready to give you a quick run down on things before ward round.'

'Thank you.' Jennifer followed Martha into a large office at the end of the corridor, feeling pleased and excited and ready to get to work. She'd really made it to the top. It all still seemed a little surreal. As she passed the door, she paused to glance at the name plaque. DEPARTMENT OF ORTHOPAEDICS AND TRAUMA. HEAD OF UNIT. DR JENNIFER THORNGATE. She'd done it!

'Dr Thorngate,' Martha said, breaking into her thoughts. 'This is Dr Edwards.'

Jennifer turned her attention away from the door to look at the man sitting behind her new desk, in her new chair. He took his time standing, as though he didn't care he'd been found riffling through her papers. There was confidence about him and she liked that. He wore dark trousers, a crisp white shirt and a colourful tie. The shirt, however, pulled slightly across his arms as he pushed on the desk with both hands as he stood. The fabric outlined two very firm and well-toned arms and she couldn't help but note how broad his shoulders were.

His hair was dark brown and his eyes were a smoky grey, filled with politeness as he came over and held out his hand. 'Dr Thorngate. Welcome to Parramatta Hospital, although I understand from your file that you actually trained here.'

'Medical school, yes.' Why did she feel as though he was the boss and she was the new recruit? 'Thank you for the welcome, Dr Edwards.'

'Please. Call me Eddie. Most of the staff do.'

'All right, Eddie. I understand you've been keeping the seat warm — literally.' She pointed to the chair he'd just vacated.

He smiled at that and the effect made her do a double-take. Nice. *Very* nice. She swallowed and forced herself to look away. 'That's right.' He turned to the secretary. 'Martha, would you mind getting refreshments? I'm sure Dr Thorngate could do with a quick cuppa before ward round.'

'Oh, I'm fine. I've already had two cups of coffee this morning.' Jennifer quickly waved his words away, wanting to get control over her equilibrium. It wasn't a common occurrence for her to be knocked off guard by a simple smile but that's exactly what Dr Edwards . . . Eddie, she corrected herself . . . had done. With firm strides, she headed around the desk.

He leaned forward a little and raised his eyebrows questioningly. 'Nerves?'

'Uh . . .' For a whole second Jennifer's mind went blank. The man really was extremely good-looking and highly personable. If everyone in her new department was like him, she wasn't going to have any trouble settling in. 'Something like that.'

Dr Edwards smiled again. 'Well, you're probably going to need to top up at some point because you have an extremely busy day ahead of you.' He didn't move. Didn't shift to the other side of the desk, as she'd expected him to. Instead, he stood there, his tall, firm body now close to hers. Close enough that she could feel the heat radiating from him and smell the fresh scent of his aftershave. Spicy and woodsy. Nice. *Very* nice.

Jennifer closed her eyes for a brief moment, forcing herself to shift into professional gear. Dr Edwards was just another colleague and while he was her equal when it came to qualifications, he wasn't head of

25

unit, which, in context of the hospital's protocols, made her his new boss.

When she next looked at him, it was to find him studying her with a degree of confusion. 'Something wrong? Caffeine headache?'

'No. No. Not at all.'

Jennifer fingered a pile of neat papers stacked on the desk as Martha left, closing the door behind her. 'Is this the usual inheritance?'

Eddie laughed. 'I've tried to clear as much of the backlog as I could but there are things I thought it better for you to deal with.'

'Then why don't you take a seat . . .' she indicated the one on the opposite side of her desk '. . . and let me know what requires my urgent attention?'

Thankfully, Eddie took the hint and moved, pulling the chair up to the edge of the desk. He was still close, still crowding her a little, but thankfully now there was a large slab of wood between them rather than just a few inches of carpet. The man radiated charm, manners and had an abundance of sex appeal. As he pointed to a piece of paper, she checked his hands. Both ringless — although that meant nothing. Was he married? Engaged? Attached in some way?

She sat there, looking at him, and realised

26

he was expecting an answer. Clearing her throat as well as her mind from distracting thoughts of her new colleague, Jennifer forced herself to concentrate.

'I'm sorry. Would you mind repeating that?'

'Is anything wrong? You seem a little . . . I don't know . . . pre-occupied, distracted.' Now he was looking at her as if she couldn't handle the job. Well, she knew she could and she was determined to show him just how well she could do it.

'No. Let's get things sorted.' When she didn't elaborate any further, Eddie repeated his initial question, which she answered knowledgeably and without vacilation.

'Right, then. The next thing that requires your immediate attention is the new research grant. It's due in on Thursday so there are only a few more days to finalise all matters.'

'Who's the supervisor on the project?'

'You.'

'Me? I've inherited a research project already?'

Eddie smiled again and once more Jennifer couldn't believe how it changed his face. Where his initial smile had been polite and welcoming, even mildly humourous, this one made his eyes sparkle, his white, straight teeth bright and inviting. Laughter lines creased at the corners of his eyes and to top off the effect, he pushed a stray lock of hair back from his forehead and shrugged his firm, broad shoulders. 'Nothing says "Welcome to the department" like inheriting a research project.'

Jennifer couldn't help but return his smile. It was so very rare that she took an instant liking to people but Dr Edwards was proving himself to be one of them. 'I guess you're right. Who's the assistant supervisor?'

'I am. As you can see, most of the details are in place. I've had Martha schedule some time for you to come across to the laboratory tomorrow afternoon so we can go over things together. That way you won't be making your decision based only on the theory and hard-copy explanations.'

'Good. Thanks for organising that.' She put the research papers in a pile. 'I'll read this tonight.'

They continued working and half an hour later, when Martha knocked on the door to say the eight-thirty ward round would start in five minutes, Jennifer looked at the large pile of papers she would be working her way through that night.

Eddie pointed to the pile. 'I'm so glad that's yours and not mine any more.'

'You don't like administration work?'

'Not my favourite thing to be doing of an evening.'

'Cuts into your social life?' She'd said the comment in an offhanded manner and when he didn't answer immediately, she looked up, surprised to find him almost frowning at her. It was on the tip of her tongue to apologise but he merely shrugged, the frown instantly disappearing.

'Something like that.'

'Dr Edwards. If you don't mind me asking, why didn't you simply take on the position of head of unit yourself? Surely it wasn't because of the amount of paperwork because, from what I've seen during the past half an hour, you're a man who knows what he's doing, knows how to run a department and is obviously very comfortable working here. I guess I'm at a loss as to why they didn't simply promote you rather than sourcing from outside the hospital.'

'Worried you think you're stepping on my toes?' His good humour was back and she wondered whether she'd imagined that little frown that had previously pierced his brow.

'A little bit. I don't like stepping on other people's toes.'

'Don't be concerned on my account.' Eddie put his big manly hand onto his chest. 'I promise you, I didn't want the job so you don't have to be worried about other staff members thinking you've come along and stepped on my toes — er . . . so to speak.' There was that smile again, the one that brightened his eyes and made Jennifer feel all funny inside. She blinked once, clearing her mind and doing her best to ignore the sensation.

'That's a relief.'

'Because of what happened at your last hospital?'

'What?'

'In Victoria, right? You were at the Royal Melbourne, correct?'

'Yes.'

'You were brought in as deputy head, promoted above someone who had worked in the hospital for years, who'd acted in that position and who'd lost out to you.'

Jennifer was taken aback at that. 'How on earth do you know about that?'

'Ah.' He touched the side of his nose. 'I have my sources.'

'Really?' Jennifer leaned back in her chair and couldn't help but cross her arms over her chest in self-defence. 'What else did your sources tell you?'

Eddie's lips twitched for a moment and he met her gaze. 'That you were the ice princess. That you were crisp and cool to everyone you met whether they were your superior or not. That you have an exceedingly high opinion of yourself and that you'll stop at next to nothing to ensure all jobs and staff perform at nothing short of an exceptional level.'

'Hmm. Not very flattering.' Her interpersonal skills were something she'd also promised herself to work on and she'd thought, given that she'd met two whole people in the department and not had one row, that she was doing quite well.

'No. Not at all.'

'Then why are you smiling at me? Aren't you concerned that I'll become crisp with you?'

Eddie laughed, the sound rich and warm. It was definitely guaranteed to melt any ice she may have been surrounding herself with. 'Not at all. In fact . . .' he leaned a little closer on the desk, his eyes intent with good humour 'I'm willing to bet you were only that cold because the rest of the staff gave you a hard time. A protective reaction, if you will. Sort of like the echidna. It only puts its prickles up when it's being attacked. We all have defence mechanisms.'

Jennifer liked his answer and nodded but wished he'd move back. The after shave he wore was rather alluring. 'We do.'

He stayed where he was for another split second, their eyes meeting. 'My sister's a little like that. I guess that's why I can recognise the trait in others.'

'S-sister?' She wished he'd move, give her some space, and as if he could read her mind, he did just that, leaning back before standing.

'She's a general surgeon.'

The intercom on Jennifer's desk buzzed and Martha announced that both of them were expected on the ward immediately. The interruption was enough to make Jennifer look away.

'Anyway, given that I was armed with this prior information of you,' Jasper continued, straightening his tie, 'I hoped that if I greeted you with a warm and endearing attitude, you wouldn't feel the need to be all ice and bristle.'

Jennifer stood and headed over to the coat rack by the door to get the new white coat which hung there for her. Eddie beat her to it and held it open for her. 'Thank you,' she said as she slipped her arms in, breathing in his warm, spicy scent again. Nice. *Very* nice. She stood there for a moment and so did he. She could feel the warmth of his body very close to hers and her heart rate started to increase. Who was this man? He smelt good, had a nice smile and firm arms . . . arms that would protect. To top it all off, he was charming and appeared to be quite honest and not afraid to speak his mind. She respected that.

She turned her head to look up at him and was surprised to find him simply watching her, his grey eyes intent. Swallowing, she found she couldn't move, mesmerised by the atmosphere that surrounded them. She was positive he could hear her heart pounding against her ribs, its rhythm increasing at the look in his eyes, but within the next second he'd shifted away, reaching for his own white coat which had hung next to hers on the rack. He turned his back as he slipped it on and Jennifer smoothed the collar of her own coat as she looked at the floor and tried desperately to forget whatever it was that had just passed between them.

'Ward round,' he said.

'Ward round.' She nodded and walked towards the door. Again his long strides had him there before her. 'Oh, I don't have my new ID badge yet. Is that going to matter?'

He angled his head. 'I think everyone's going to know who you are.' He took his own ID badge out of his coat pocket and clipped it on. It had his picture on it, his name and title. 'Everyone should have theirs on so you'll be able to learn their names, ranks and serial numbers.' He chuckled at his own joke but Jennifer hadn't really heard what he'd said as her eyes were intent on his own badge.

'Jasper? Your name is Jasper?'

'Yes. Jasper Edwards.'

'Jasper Edwards?' She said the name slowly and then closed her eyes and shook her head. '*You're* Jasper Edwards?'

'Is something wrong?'

'You don't by any chance have a couple of gorgeous four-year-old daughters with lovely blonde ringlets and blue eyes called Lilly and Lola, do you?'

Jasper's puzzled expression slid from his face to be replaced by one of total incredulity, his eyes wide with disbelief, yet he kept his voice controlled and calm. 'How on earth do you know that?'

CHAPTER TWO

'I knew it.' Jennifer shook her head and walked past him, not even bothering to look at Martha as she strode down the corridor.

'Knew what?' Jasper was beside her in an instant, those long strides of his eating up the distance with ease. 'How do you know all these things?'

'I knew she couldn't resist meddling in my life but this . . . this is pure cunning.' Jennifer was muttering, talking more to herself than to Jasper, but he was listening quite intently as he kept pace with her.

'Who? Who are you talking about? How do you know about my girls?'

Jennifer stopped walking and turned to face him. 'Sara.' Her tone was cross and after shaking her head she continued on her way.

'Sara? Matt's wife?'

'Yes, Matt's wife. How many Saras do you know?'

'A few. That's not the point. Obviously you know Sara.'

'Yes, and obviously we spoke on the phone last week.'

'What?' Jasper couldn't believe how bewildering this woman was. She was smart, gorgeous and his new boss. To top it all off, she knew about his daughters. It wasn't that people around the hospital didn't know he had children, they did, but Jasper had worked hard to keep his private life as far away from the hospital world as possible.

When he'd started dating again two years ago, he'd made a pact with himself to protect the girls as much as possible. He'd started out by not wanting to date anyone who worked at the hospital but as he spent the majority of his time there — and the rest at home with the twins — he realised it was virtually impossible to meet anyone who wasn't associated in some way with the medical profession. To ensure the girls were protected, he'd compartmentalised his life and things had been going swimmingly . . . until now. If Jennifer knew Sara then his two worlds had just collided with a very loud bang and he wasn't quite sure what to do next.

'What do you mean we spoke on the phone? When?'

'The other day when you called Sara's house. The line was bad. Remember?'

'That was you?' His eyebrows shot up in surprise. 'Why did you say you were Sara?'

'I didn't. I told you it wasn't Sara but you couldn't hear me.'

He nodded. 'The line was bad.'

They weren't far from the ward now and Jennifer was having difficulties slotting Jasper 'call me Eddie' Edwards into a nice, neat compartment. He didn't fit under the 'work colleague' banner, neither did he fit under the 'friend' banner, and in the past those were the only two banners she'd had. Knowing he was a friend of Sara's automatically connected her professional and private lives together and she didn't like that at all. She needed to get this sorted out and *now*.

She came to a halt and grabbed Jasper's arm, pulling him into a small nook near a drinking fountain.

'Look. I don't like it when my personal and private lives mix.'

'Neither do I.'

'Good. Then Sara can just forget her wild ideas and we can simply work together as colleagues and nothing more. Agreed?'

Jasper frowned. 'What wild ideas? What on earth are you talking about?'

'Sara!'

'I've gathered that much. I've also realised you're the friend who's been staying with Sara for this past week.'

'Yes.' It was her turn to frown.

'The girls came home on Thursday, after spending the day with Sara, talking about Sara's friend, Jen. I'm guessing you're Jen.'

'You really are very smart, Dr Edwards. Good to know you can connect the dots so easily.' Her tone was laced with light sarcasm.

'Hey. Why are you cross with me? It's just a coincidence, that's all.'

'Yes, but one I could have at least prepared myself for.'

'You're talking in riddles again.'

'Sara's been trying to get me to date again.'

Jasper's eyebrows hit his hairline at her words. 'Sara wants to set us up!'

'Now you're getting the picture.' Jennifer looked down at her clenched hands for a moment, then lifted her head, raising her chin with a hint of defiance. Jasper found he liked the action but pushed that thought aside for now. 'We were talking about you the other day. After you'd called.'

'You were?' Should he be worried? Jennifer had already mentioned that Sara was trying to set them up. Had Sara been touting his good points? He waited.

'I was trying to figure out the loose family connection.' She waved her words away and shook her head as though a little embarrassed by her confession. 'Anyway, I asked her where you worked and she quickly changed the subject. You see, she knew I was coming to work here — in this department. She knew you worked here so why do you think that a woman as bright and intelligent as Sara wouldn't tell us about each other?'

'I don't know. It slipped her mind?'

'Do you really believe that? If you do, you don't know Sara all that well.'

'Wait a minute. Why does she want you to start dating again?'

Jennifer visibly bristled and squared her shoulders. 'That is none of your business, Dr Edwards.'

'I think it is, especially if I've been chosen as the guy to get you off the blocks.' His good humour was beginning to reassert itself. A flush came to her cheeks at his words and he realised it caused her eyes to sparkle like the deep blue of the ocean. Her black hair was pulled back into a tight bun and for a startling moment he wondered what she'd look like with it flowing loose and free around her shoulders.

'Dr Edwards, all you need to know is that I don't date my staff, even if I *was* ready to "get off the blocks", as you so eloquently put it. End of discussion.' With that, she turned and walked into the ward, her back firm as she put all thoughts of her new, sexy colleague out of her mind.

It was easier said than done and she was very aware of him as she undertook her first ward round. It was the one time she should be exhibiting total professionalism. She was the new boss. This was what she'd been waiting for for so long and now that it was here all she seemed conscious of was where Jasper Edwards was standing. Her body seemed to have tuned itself to him and even when he was out of sight, his fresh scent worked its way into her synapses and continued to tease her to distraction.

Twice she had an intern waiting patiently for her to answer a question. The whole entourage, which was made up of medical students, interns, registrars and her fellow consultants — including Jasper — watched her intently, waiting for her words of wisdom. The problem was she had no idea what the initial questions had been, all due to her awareness of 'Eddie'.

Jennifer was cross with herself for not maintaining total control. She'd had to freeze out the world before and she could do it again, especially if it meant she avoided making a fool of herself in front of her staff. Sara may have thought Jasper Edwards up to the job of melting her hardened heart but Jennifer knew better. She'd been called the ice queen at her old hospital and she wasn't at all perturbed about continuing that name here — especially if it meant colleagues like Jasper Edwards kept their distance.

After they'd completed the ward round, Jennifer was about to head back to her office to take another look at her schedule for the day when the clinical nurse consultant called her over.

'There's a call for you, Dr Thorngate.'

'Thank you.' Jennifer took the receiver to discover it was Martha.

'Your morning heads of unit meeting has been cancelled. Professors Dorian and Fitzgibbon have flu and won't be in.'

'It seems to be chasing me,' she murmured absent-mindedly.

'Pardon?' Martha asked.

'It was going around in Melbourne and I managed to avoid it. It doesn't matter. Does this mean I head to clinic?'

'Yes. Eddie will show you around if you're not sure where to go.'

'Thank you.' There was no point in telling her new secretary that she wasn't about to rely on 'Eddie' for anything. If she got lost, she'd ask someone else for directions. After all, she was a woman and if there was one thing women knew how to do, it was to ask for directions.

'I've rebooked you in to have your hospital identification photograph taken at one o'clock, which should give you enough time to finish in clinic,' Martha continued. Jennifer listened to her secretary, pleased Martha was not only highly trained but communicative as well. It was sort of strange having a secretary all to herself, where as deputy head of unit at her last hospital she'd had to share secretarial support with three other consultants.

When she'd finished on the phone, Jennifer closed her eyes for a moment and took a deep, calming breath. Her eyes snapped open when that now familiar spicy scent wound itself about her senses once more.

Without turning around, she said, 'Is there something I can help you with, Dr Edwards?'

'How did you know I was here?' he asked softly.

'I'm good like that.' She turned slightly to see him lounging in a chair, his hands fiddling with a pen he'd just picked up off the desk. He was handsome. She'd give him that. Those eyes of his, which were now watching her intently, were the most amazing colour and Jennifer had the feeling she could lose herself in them quite easily . . . But she was stronger than that. She could quite easily resist. Straightening her shoulders and lifting her chin with a hint of defiance, she waited for him to continue.

'Better than you were during ward round, I hope,' he stated with a quirk of an eyebrow.

His words put her on the defensive and she crossed her arms, her tone crisp and concise. 'Meaning?'

He put the pen down and lifted his hands, palms out towards her. 'Nothing. Just teasing.'

Jennifer looked down her nose at him, needing to put him in his place because then she'd hopefully be able to gain better control over her own wayward emotions. 'Well, I'd kindly ask you to keep comments such as those to yourself in future.'

'Ah, and there she is. The ice queen who terrified medical students, interns and registrars at her previous hospital. When I met you this morning, I thought Ted McGinchley had been wrong, you were so sweet and charming. Although I guess if people are rubbing you up the wrong way you're bound to hit defensive mode sooner rather than later.'

'Let me guess, you enjoy rubbing people up the wrong way. Sparking a reaction and having a good chuckle about it later?'

'I don't chuckle about it. Sometimes, though, ruffling a few feathers makes life a little more exciting, don't you think?' His look was direct, his gaze unwavering, and Jennifer found herself unable to move for a moment. Her mind also seemed to have been wiped blank yet again and she had no idea what they'd just been talking about. She needed to regain control again, and fast.

'Well, if you don't want anything, I'll head up to clinic.' She turned and walked toward the ward doors, thanking the CNC on her way out. She knew Jasper was beside her, those long legs of his covering the distance without a problem.

'I thought you had a meeting.'

'It's been cancelled.'

'Right.' They fell into an uncomfortable silence as they walked along the corridor towards clinic. Jasper wasn't quite sure why he'd been teasing Jennifer. He guessed it wasn't good to antagonise the woman who could give the green light to certain projects he was contemplating. As a trained ortho-

44

paedic consultant, Jasper was one of two surgeons employed full time by the hospital. Jennifer was the other. Usually consultants spent a certain number of hours at the hospital and the rest in their private practices, but as Jasper's main interest was in trauma medicine, working in the hospital full time gave him the opportunity to continue being an orthopaedic trauma specialist. Jennifer, however, was now in control of the department's budget so he'd do well to remember that.

He knew on a psychological level he should try to distance himself from her. He'd heard from his colleague in Melbourne that Jennifer Thorngate didn't care about anything except her work. It was no wonder he'd been expecting the dragon lady, and he was still trying to get over his initial surprise at the way she'd smiled and laughed with him earlier that morning. He'd been even more surprised to discover he'd *liked* the way she looked, the way her eyes sparkled with mirth and the way he appeared instantly drawn to her.

He'd been further intrigued to learn not only about the connection with Sara but that Sara was trying to get Jennifer to date again. Again? What had happened in Jennifer's past to make that a necessity? Had she lost someone close to her? Was that why she lived only for the job and nothing else? He, of all people, knew what it was like to feel the agony of losing a loved one and relying on work to get you through, but he also knew it was important to get back into life or you could end up losing *yourself.* If he hadn't had the twins, he wasn't sure he would have survived Elisha's death, but he'd had to go on living, raising his beautiful girls, and he was glad he had. Sure, it wasn't easy but life was about the journey, not rushing to the end.

However much he was intrigued by the new head of unit, he'd do well to keep the relationship strictly professional. She'd met his daughters. There was nothing he could do about that. He might even see her from time to time at the many barbecues and big family gatherings Sara loved to organize, and he could deal with that, too. But that would be the extent of their personal contact and if she was going to freeze him out, well, he just might let her.

They entered the clinic without another word spoken between them, as though they'd both been making firm resolutions and were now intent on keeping them. Jasper politely introduced her to the outpatient clerical staff as well as the nursing staff and then picked up a file and called his first patient through.

Clinic was as busy as she'd expected and she was glad she'd been able to help rather than being stuck in a meeting. The only glimpse she had of Jasper was when he was escorting a patient into his consulting room while she'd been escorting one out.

'Professional,' she whispered to herself as she went to have her identification photograph taken. She could handle anything so long as she maintained her professional persona.

It was well after seven o'clock when Jennifer finally swapped her white coat for her suit jacket and large winter coat. She had a briefcase full of work to keep her company that evening and was ready to head back to Sara's place.

As she walked to the front of the hospital, she heard someone call her name and turned around to see Jasper heading in her direction. She prepared herself for the next onslaught of what he called teasing. She hoped he wouldn't. She was worn out and just wanted to be left alone. What she hadn't expected were the tingles that assailed her body as he drew closer. She ignored them and went on the defensive instead.

'Dr Edwards.' She nodded curtly. 'Forgot

to say something else this morning? Perhaps an extra insult that you just wanted to get off your chest before you left for the night so you could sleep in peace?'

'Ooh, and there's that sarcasm of yours. Right in my face and making me want to say something to definitely rub you up the wrong way.'

Jennifer stared defiantly at him for a moment then the tension seemed to flood out of both of them and they laughed. 'I'm sorry,' she said, shaking her head.

'I am, too. I guess I didn't make it easy for you today.'

Jennifer shrugged. 'I've had worse first days.' She pointed to the briefcase he held in his hand. 'You're a bit late to be heading home.'

'It happens. Are you heading to your car?'

'Yes.'

'I'll walk with you.' With that he waved to the security guard who was on his way over. 'I'll walk with Dr Thorngate,' he said, and Jennifer was left with no choice but to go with him.

'At least it's not raining.' She tried to make small talk.

'I guess, coming from Melbourne where it drizzles all day long in winter, Sydney might be seen as an improvement.'

'I guess but I remember quite clearly what winter is like in Parramatta.'

'Of course. I keep forgetting you know your way around here.' He paused then asked, 'Is that how you know Sara? She only said she had an old friend staying with her,' he added.

'We've been friends since high school.'

'I remember now. She calls you Jen most of the time, right?'

'Yes.'

'Do you prefer Jennifer or Jen?'

'Jennifer at work. Only my closest friends call me Jen.'

Jasper nodded but didn't make any further comment. She pointed to a blue Jaguar Mark II. 'This is me.'

'This is *your* car?'

'I just said as much. Why? What's wrong?'

'It's just that . . . well . . . usually women don't drive classic cars like this.'

'That's a very chauvinistic comment, Jasper. I'm sure you'd like your daughters to have an appreciation of fine cars.'

'Well, yes, of course. Sorry.'

'Don't be. I'm used to that sort of reaction from men.'

'Have you had it long?'

'About eight years.' She took a deep breath, looked down at the ground then met his eyes, the car park's artificial lighting accentuating his angular jaw and straight nose. 'It belonged to my fiancé. He died of cancer.' There. It was out. She'd learned to say the words matter-of-factly, removing all emotion whenever she brought up Arturo.

Jasper nodded slowly. 'Why are you telling me this? I thought you liked to keep your private life private.'

'I do, but let's face it, Jasper. Sara seems intent on getting the two of us together so no doubt she's planning some party or get-together soon and we'll be forced to mix. She'll also let slip details about my past, just as she's told me about yours.'

'So you've said.'

'It was only the basics. She probably thinks that because we've both lost someone to cancer that we have a lot in common.'

Jasper scratched his head. 'She thinks that grief can bring people together?'

'You know Sara. Her mind works in a way that is still a mystery to most top neurologists.'

He smiled at that, hearing the love she had for her friend in her voice. 'And this is why she wants you to start dating again? Because you drive your deceased fiancé's car?'

Jennifer had to smile. 'It's not just the car.'

'It shouldn't be. It's an amazing car.'

'It's a money guzzler.' She stroked the bonnet lovingly. 'But I don't begrudge one single penny.'

'Let me guess. It makes you feel close to him?'

'Art. Arturo — that was his name and, yes, it does.'

Jasper nodded. 'I'm like that with my bedroom. My wife decorated it in her own special style — she was an artist. Even now, three years later, even though I know I've moved on emotionally, I still love being in that room.'

'It's like looking through an old photo album and remembering the good times.'

'Yes. Exactly.' Jasper smiled at her. 'My mother thinks it's morbid to leave the room the way it is but I wouldn't change it for anything, just as I'm sure you're not going to get rid of this car.'

'No. She's a part of me.'

Jasper was silent for a moment before asking quietly, 'Would you mind giving me a ride home?' He looked longingly at the car as she'd seen so many men do over the years.

'Don't you have your car here?'

'I do, but it can stay here overnight. Classic cars such as this little beauty . . .' he stroked the bonnet '. . . don't come along every day.'

'So you want me to drive you home just so you can ride in her? How will you get to work in the morning?'

'I don't live far. I can walk.'

'What if it's raining?'

'Then I'll use an umbrella.'

Jennifer smiled, liking his logical answer. 'Are you sure?'

'Of course. I am a man who knows his own mind . . . most of the time,' he added with a grin.

'All right, then.' She shifted her briefcase to the other hand and pulled the keys out of her pocket. She contemplated her decision for a whole split second before holding them out to him. 'As it's not that far to your place, would you like to drive her?'

Jasper's eyes almost popped out of his head and Jennifer couldn't help but laugh. 'Are you serious?'

'Of course I am. And I *am* a woman who knows her own mind.'

'You'd let a complete stranger drive your very special car?'

'First of all,' she said as she unlocked the driver's side, then opened the back door to put her briefcase in, 'you're not a complete stranger, Jasper. Secondly, we may be new colleagues but you've known Sara for years, as have I, and I'm sure we both know that Sara is very careful about who she gives her loyalty to. And, thirdly, I've met your daughters and as a father you would no doubt be a careful driver, given you'd often be carrying precious cargo in the back.'

'Any other reasons?' He was teasing her, she could tell by the slight twitch of his lips. It was interesting how she'd picked up on that so quickly but, then again, he'd teased her quite a few times today.

'Yes.' She held out the keys to him. 'Because I can tell you really want to.'

Jasper nodded and this time took the keys from her, holding them as though they were precious jewels. Jennifer headed around to the passenger side and watched as Jasper took off his coat and placed it carefully on the back seat next to his briefcase before sliding smoothly behind the wheel. He leaned across and opened the passenger door for her, then put the key in the ignition and placed his hands on the leather steering-wheel.

Jennifer was very pleased when he didn't start the car straight away but instead seemed to be taking his time, looking around, checking out where the lights were, the windscreen wipers, reading the dials.

His hands caressed the steering-wheel in the same way Art had done and she smiled at that. She loved this car, there was no doubt about that, and it wasn't only for sentimental reasons but she had to laugh at the way men were almost hypnotised by it.

'She's like a grand old lady, perfect in every minor detail. What's her name?'

'What makes you think she has a name?' Jennifer was instantly amused.

'Come on. Tell me her name.'

'Why do men name their cars? I've never understood that.'

'What's her name?' Jasper reiterated insistently. 'I know she has one because if your fiancé loved her as much as I think he did, he would have named her.'

Jennifer rolled her eyes. 'Miss Chief.'

'Mischief?'

'No. Miss Chief.' She said the two words slowly. 'But she can be a bit mischievous at times.'

Jasper wiggled his fingers as he reached for the ignition and sighed as the car purred to life. 'Glorious.'

'Do you two want to be alone?' Jennifer laughed and clipped her seat belt on. She hadn't been a passenger in this car for a very long time and it felt kind of nice to be driven around in it once more. She settled more comfortably into the leather seat, ready to enjoy being chauffeured.

Jasper drove as carefully as she'd expected him to and within a few minutes he was pulling up outside a large two-storey house. 'She's perfect. Just perfect.'

'I'm glad you think so.' Jennifer undid her seat belt and pointed to his house. 'This is where you live?'

'It is.'

'You're lucky to be so close to the hospital. I've been looking for a place for quite some time but with no luck.'

'Can't find anywhere close?' He'd switched off the engine but kept his hands on the wheel, not quite ready to part with the sensation of such a classic car.

'No, which is why I'm still at Sara's. If you know of any decent-sized apartments in the area, would you mind letting me know?'

'The house two doors down is for sale,' Jasper remarked, pointing.

Jennifer wrinkled her nose and shook her head. 'I'm not interested in a house.'

'It's only two bedroomed, more like a cottage really, and, besides, an apartment complex would mean you'd have to park Miss Chief in a shared garage or, worse, on the street. The house down the road has a nice large garage just perfect for this regal beauty.' He paused for a moment, unsure whether he was doing the right thing or not. 'I know the owner. Want me to get him to contact you?'

'Well . . .' It was all a bit sudden but he did have a point. 'I was looking for an apartment with a private garage.'

'You won't find one around here. Not close to the hospital. Check out the house,' he pushed again. 'Just go for a look around. See if you like it.' He shrugged. 'I'll even come with you if you want.'

'You'd do that?' She was surprised by the sweet gesture and it made her realise that Jasper Edwards was indeed someone she might be able to trust. *Might.*

'It's the least I can do after you've let me drive Miss Chief.'

'Hmm. Maybe I should remember that. Whenever I need Jasper to do something, I'll just let him drive my car.'

'I'm an easy sell,' he replied with a chuckle, and reluctantly climbed out of the car. Jennifer followed suit and walked around to the driver's side. 'Thanks, Jennifer. She really was an amazing drive.'

'My pleasure.' And she realised it was. It had been good to share her love of the car with someone who really appreciated it. They stood there for a few moments, looking at each other, before Jasper seemed to realise he should move. He collected his coat and briefcase.

'I guess I'll see you tomorrow.'

'I guess you will,' she replied.

'The second day is always better than the first,' he said as he walked over his front lawn.

'I'll look forward to it, then.'

Jasper nodded slowly, heading into the shadows. 'So will I.'

CHAPTER THREE

For the next two weeks, Jennifer started to find her feet in her new job. As good as his word, Jasper was professional yet polite when he showed her around the research laboratory and introduced her to various members of staff. She felt comfortable going to him with questions or concerns she had, just trying to get a feel for what had transpired before her arrival.

When she'd arrived home at Sara's house that first night, she hadn't said a word to Sara about meeting Jasper. Sara had hedged a little, asking her how the day had gone — had she met any new and exciting people? Jennifer had played it cool, deciding to keep Sara in the dark for a bit longer. Instead, she'd eaten her dinner, played a board game with Sara's boys for half an hour and then headed to her room to settle down to the contents of her briefcase.

The evenings were usually hectic, with

Jennifer not leaving the hospital until very late, only to be back bright and early the following morning.

'You're working too hard,' Jasper told her one Thursday evening.

'I'm the boss. I need to work hard. How can I ask more of my staff if I don't give one hundred and ten per cent?'

Jasper eased himself into the chair opposite her desk and shook his head, tut-tutting. 'You're still working too hard and you're not going to inspire anyone if you end up sick. Or haven't you noticed the bug which seems to be sweeping its way through the hospital?'

'Of course I've noticed. Why do you think I'm working so hard?' Her words had come out defensively and harshly, and the instant they were out she closed her eyes and sighed. 'I'm sorry, Jasper.' She hung her head for a moment, rubbing her fingers in tiny circles around her temples before looking at him once more. He was such a nice man and had been nothing but supportive during her time there so far. He didn't deserve to incur her frustrations and insecurities. 'I'm just eager to get all this work done and up to date so I can settle down into a more normal rhythm.'

'Filling in for other staff and working

yourself to death isn't going to accomplish anything.'

'Then what do you suggest I do?' She indicated her desk, piled high with paper-work, as she spoke. Jasper heard a hint of mild desperation in her tone. 'I was chosen for this job. It's what I've been working towards for a very long time and I don't want the powers that be to think I'm incompetent and —'

'They won't think that,' Jasper interrupted as he stood and walked towards her. He stood behind her chair and placed his hands on her shoulders. She jumped when he touched her but he kept his hands still for a moment and the warmth he generated started to flow into her tired and exhausted trapezius. 'You are doing an incredible job and no one is going to blame you for taking a night off and relaxing a little rather than beating yourself with a stick and wearing sackcloth and ashes.'

Her lips twitched at his words. 'Sackcloth and ashes?' She was working very hard at ignoring the way her body responded so readily to his nearness. There was something about him which she found highly attractive . . . in fact, if she was honest, there was a *lot* about him she found highly attractive and keeping her distance, making sure their working relationship was that and nothing more, was the only thing which had helped keep her unwanted attraction to Jasper in check.

'You know what I mean. Listen. Why don't we get out of here and go grab a bite to eat?'

'But what about your girls? Don't you need to get home to them?' Jennifer was concerned for both Lilly and Lola, not wanting to take their father's time away from them but, really, she was more concerned with being alone with Jasper for any great stretch of time. In fact, they were alone now . . . here . . . in her office . . . the rest of the staff either on duty or off home. They were more alone here than they would be at a crowded, busy restaurant.

Jasper's hands were moving slowly, working their magic and beginning to unknot her shoulders. She would relax too much with him like this . . . secluded in her office. She needed to move. She needed to put distance between them. She needed to . . .

'Mmm.' Jennifer heard herself moan as he continued to massage. It was so good. So nice. So warm and caring. So . . . evocative.

At that realisation, she pushed away from her desk, almost knocking Jasper over in her haste to put as much distance between them as possible. Her eyes were wide, her breathing doubling in an instant from its previous relaxed rate, and she started fidgeting with the papers she'd almost knocked off her desk.

'Jennifer?'

'Er . . . Nothing. I mean, thanks for the massage. Did you say something about dinner?' She opened her drawer and pulled out her handbag. 'We can take my car if you like.' Focusing on searching for her car keys and quite unable to look at him, she tried to pull herself together. When he didn't say anything, she knew she had to meet his gaze. 'Unless you do need to get home to your girls. Of course you do. It's all right. Sara usually keeps leftovers in the fridge for me so it's no trouble to —'

'Jennifer.' He interrupted her again, a smile twitching at his lips. 'The girls will already be in bed by now and are well cared for. Of course we can take your car, if you'd prefer, but just relax. It's only dinner.'

'Right. I know. I guess your words are finally starting to sink in.' she walked over to the coat rack and swapped her white coat for her warm jacket. 'Do you know anywhere good that's also close?'

'I do.' Jasper walked to the door. 'I'll just get my things from my office. Won't be a moment.'

'Great. Sounds great.' She watched him walk away, his stride strong and purposeful as he made his way down the corridor to where his own office was. When he was out of sight, she closed her eyes and started to reflect over what had just happened. Jasper's touch. The way he'd looked at her, that cute little smile of his playing about his lips. The warmth of his hands. The nearness of his body. The scent of him overpowering her senses.

It had been so incredibly long since she'd been seriously attracted to another man that she wasn't at all sure how to behave. 'You can do this. You can do this,' she kept telling herself as she locked up. 'It's just dinner . . . with a friend. Nothing more.'

But as Jasper made his way back up the corridor towards her, she knew she was lying to herself. Spending time one on one with Jasper probably wasn't the best idea in the world but, she had to admit, she was rather curious about him. Sure, Sara had filled in a few of the gaps but *she* had definitely been intrigued by him, even before she'd known his true identity.

'Ready?'

'As ready as I'll ever be,' she replied, and they headed out of the hospital. Jasper walked with her to her car and this time refused the keys when she offered them to him.

'I'll navigate.' His deep words washed over her as she exited the car park and for a split second she wondered if he was offering to navigate more than the car. Was Jasper also willing to navigate her through the rocky waters of moving on with her life? Of course she'd moved on in a professional capacity but emotionally she knew she'd held onto the past for too long. It was one of the reasons she'd returned to Parramatta. She needed to lay her past to rest once and for all. She needed to move on. To date. To find someone else to share her time with. Otherwise she'd end up all alone . . . And she didn't want to be alone.

Jasper navigated extremely well and after she'd parked Miss Chief, they walked the short block to the dining district in the main street of Parramatta. 'The world is your oyster . . . literally,' Jasper said, pointing to a seafood restaurant. 'What do you feel in the mood for?'

'Huh?' Jennifer was mildly startled by his question. She'd been intent on walking beside him, intent on trying not to get too close that their hands touched, intent on calming her nerves because she was out with a man . . . and not just any man at that.

Jasper only chuckled. 'Good to see your brain's starting to relax. How about here?' He pointed at a restaurant that served café cuisine but also a large variety of foods. Their menus were printed up as a newspaper which you had to open to read. Jennifer was impressed with the gimmick and after they were seated and had trawled through the menu, deciding what to eat, she eased back in her chair and sighed, a smile on her face.

'That's better,' Jasper declared.

'What is?'

'You.'

'Me?'

'Yes. *Now* you're starting to relax. It's good to see.'

Jennifer nodded. 'You're right. I do tend to push myself too hard, too fast. Thanks for making me get out, Jasper.'

'Although I have to confess . . .' he leaned a little closer, his elbows on the table, his eyes focused on hers '. . . I thought I was doing a good job of relaxing you back in your office.'

Jennifer blinked once and simply stared at him. Did he mean what she thought he meant? She swallowed, unable to speak for a moment.

'Your shoulders are far too tight. I'd be more than happy to act as your remedial massage therapist if it's going to help.' He waggled his eyebrows up and down in a suggestive manner, that gorgeous smile that managed to melt her heart touching his lips.

'Uh . . . I don't . . . Uh . . .' She cleared her throat '. . . know if that would be the . . . er . . . best idea.'

'Why not? You were certainly enjoying it back in your office.' His voice was so rich, so deep, and it wasn't just washing over her any more — it was washing through her.

'Jasper.' She knew now he'd been well aware of the effects he'd been having on her, was *still* having on her. She decided not to play games any longer. 'We can't. We're colleagues.'

'True, and no doubt we're better off maintaining a friendship, but that doesn't change the fact that you're the first woman I have been seriously attracted to in a very long time.'

'Jasper.' His name was a tortured whisper as she shook her head. 'Don't say things like that.'

'Why not? It's the truth and I've found it a good policy always to stick to it wherever possible.'

'So you're . . . you're . . . attra—' She stopped as the waiter delivered their food. They both smiled their thanks and when they were left alone Jennifer found it difficult to look at him again. He was attracted to her and he'd admitted it. Just like that. She had a feeling that she'd been out of the dating loop for far too long if this was the way things were now done.

'You have your family. I have . . .' She paused.

'You have what?' His words soft and slightly probing.

Jennifer sat up a little straighter and squared her shoulders. When she spoke, she met his eyes. 'I have my job and while that might not sound like much to some, I've worked extremely hard to get to where I am and I want to enjoy it.'

Jasper opened his mouth as though he was about to say something else but then changed his mind at the last second. 'Fair enough. Let's eat while it's still hot.'

She blinked once, a little surprised at his acquiescence, but decided it wasn't good to look a gift horse in the mouth. 'It looks delicious,' she remarked.

'Me? Or the food?' Jasper asked, that teasing glint back in his eyes.

'The food.' She pointed her fork at him.

'Now, cut it out. We're just going to be friends.'

'Why?'

Jennifer's expression and her tone were quite serious. 'Because I don't have many.'

Jasper nodded as though accepting her answer. 'Fair enough.' He raised his glass and held it out to hers. 'Friends,' he toasted as they chinked glasses before raising them to their lips — both of them hoping they'd be able to stick to this resolve.

'I feel like I hardly see you,' Sara complained when Jennifer called her late on Friday afternoon to let her know she wouldn't be there for dinner again.

'It's only because I'm trying to get everything settled as quickly as possible. The workload will even out soon enough and I won't be burning the candle at both ends.' Or having impromptu dinners with Jasper, she added silently. She'd had such a great time with him, simply being out on her own with a man whose company she enjoyed. He was smart, funny and not at all difficult to look at.

'But what about trying to find an apartment?' Sara's words brought her thoughts back to the present. 'I mean, don't get me wrong, Jen, you're more than welcome to stay here for as long as you need to, but I know you want to get a place of your own, have your own space. How are you going to have time to do that when you're stuck in that hospital during daylight hours?'

'Actually, Ja— er, a colleague has told me of a place for sale which is close to the hospital.'

'Great.'

'I'm meeting the owner in half an hour,' she said, checking her watch.

'The owner? Not the real-estate agent?'

'It's a private sale.'

Sara's tone was instantly wary. 'I don't know, Jen. I don't like the sound of this. It all sounds a bit . . . I don't know . . . dodgy.'

There was a knock at Jennifer's door and she looked up, placing her hand over the receiver, and called, 'Come in.' A moment later Jasper walked into the room. Jennifer ignored the little spark of pleasure at seeing him. Those sparks were becoming all too familiar of late.

'Should I come back?' he asked, but she shook her head and beckoned him in. She pointed to the phone and mouthed, 'Sara.' Jasper nodded and sat down, his eyes starting to twinkle.

'Have you said anything?' he asked softly.

Jennifer shook her head but smiled at him. Jasper felt the now familiar hit to his solar plexus. It occurred whenever she smiled like that and in his opinion, when he didn't see her all that often, he started to miss it. Last night, though, he'd had a fantastic time. For the first time in a long time he'd felt happy, free and single. Being the father of two meant he didn't often get that much time alone, especially to spend it with an intelligent woman like Jennifer.

He had to hand it to her. She was a good administrator as well as a brilliant surgeon and while she may have ruffled a few feathers since her arrival, it had all been necessary, and he'd backed her up one hundred per cent. The fact that she was undeniably beautiful, with the most sparkling bright blue eyes, was an added bonus.

'Don't worry about me,' Jennifer said into the receiver, then switched the phone to the loudspeaker so Jasper could hear what Sara was saying. 'The colleague who's recommended this property has known the owner for a long time.'

'Sure, but you hardly know your colleague.' Sara's concern was evident. 'You've only been at the hospital for a few weeks. Perhaps you should get Jasper to check out your colleague?'

'Jasper? You mean Lilly and Lola's dad? What does he have to do with anything?' She grinned at Jasper and winked at him. Neither of them had said a word to Sara that they'd figured out her little plan and it was starting to drive poor Sara absolutely crazy.

Sara sighed with exasperation. 'Jasper works at the hospital.'

'He does?'

'Yes, and I can't understand why you haven't met him yet. He's in your department.'

'Why didn't you tell me before now?'

'Well, I, er . . . Well I didn't want to . . . er . . . influence you or prejudice you.'

'Against a colleague?'

'You *must* have met him by now. You *must* have. He's tall, dark and handsome and he told me he was expecting a new boss in the department.'

'Does he know I'm your friend?'

'No. I didn't say anything to him either, and when he picked up the girls yesterday afternoon I tried to sort of hedge around to see if he'd met you, but he didn't say a word.'

'Why is it all such a big secret? I mean, why not let either of us know before I started in the department?'

'Because . . .' Sara sighed again. 'Well, because I thought he might be perfect for you.'

'Perfect, eh? In what way?' Jennifer's eyes met Jasper's before she looked him over, taking in the chambray shirt which fitted over his torso to perfection, highlighting those perfect arms and broad shoulders. His tie was his university tie and as she looked him over he brushed his hand through his hair. When her eyes met his again she could see the humour displayed there as well as a veiled hint of desire, indicating he'd enjoyed her appraisal. He even gave her a little wink, forcing her to ignore the way her heart rate increased at that one look from him. Friends. They'd decided to be friends.

'You know what I mean.' Sara's exasperation was starting to build to an all time high. 'Perfect for you to date.'

'Oh, I see.' She couldn't help but chuckle as Jasper put one hand behind his head and the other on his hip, striking a pose. The man was so free and funny. She liked it.

'Why are you laughing? Jenn-i-fer?' Sara's tone was dark and Jennifer knew she was in trouble because Sara rarely used her full name.

'Hi, Sara,' Jasper said, his tone warm and inviting.

'Jasper? You're there!'

'I'm here.'

'Have you got me on speaker?' Sara demanded.

'Yes.'

'Jennifer Alyce Thorngate, you are in a massive amount of trouble when I see you next, and don't even think of staying at the hospital until two o'clock in the morning because I'll be waiting for you when you get in.'

'If you say so, Sara Elizabeth Jones.'

'So I take it you two have met and figured out I wanted to get you together so you thought you'd have a little bit of payback, right?'

'Right,' they said in unison. At that moment Jasper's pager went off and he checked the number.

'A and E.'

Jennifer nodded. The next moment her own pager beeped. 'Listen, Sara. We've got to go.' She checked the information on her own pager. A and E. 'An emergency's just come in.'

'A likely story,' Sara grunted. 'OK, but, listen, get Jasper to check out that colleague who wants you to buy the house.'

'*I'm* the colleague,' Jasper told her as he stood. 'The house two doors down from mine is for sale.'

'Oh.' Sara was surprised and then Jennifer heard smugness enter her tone. 'Oh, well, in that case, go right ahead.'

'I'll see you later, Sara.' Jennifer rang off, rolling her eyes as she picked up her stethoscope.

'What?' Jasper asked.

'Did you hear her tone?'

'What tone?' They headed out of her office and down the corridor.

'That smug tone of hers that says, "Ooh, Jasper and Jen will be living within two houses of each other and working together and spending so much time together that my matchmaking efforts will work and I can take the credit for them getting together." *That* tone.'

'Oh. Well maybe Sara's right?'

Jennifer stopped short. 'What? No. I've told you I'm not re—'

Jasper laughed and beckoned for her to follow. 'I'm only teasing. Gee, you're an easy mark. Come on. Let's see what sort of mess has come into A and E that we need to fix up.'

They rounded the corner into A and E and walked over to Maryanne, the orthopaedic registrar, who was expectantly waiting for them. 'What's going on?' Jasper asked.

'There's been a multiple MVA reported. Ambulances are on their way in, and reports regarding the number of casualties and possible injuries.' Maryanne directed her comments to Jasper and then to Jennifer and then back to him. It was as though she wasn't quite sure who was in charge. Well, Jennifer knew it was up to her to make sure everyone in this hospital knew exactly *who* was in charge of Orthopaedics.

'Right. Jasper.' She turned to face him. 'Once *Triage Sister* has organised the patients, I want you and two of the registrars to take the most extensive of the multiple trauma cases, which will no doubt include a pelvic fracture.' She quirked an eyebrow at him. 'I've heard you're the expert when it comes to them.'

Jasper inclined his head in a sort of bow, acknowledging her words. Jennifer turned to Maryanne. 'Have you called anyone else in?'

'Louise and Allan were just finishing their shifts so I've asked them to stay.'

Jennifer nodded. 'You're with me, Maryanne, and the service registrar on duty as well. Make sure any interns are being put to good use. I don't want to see anyone standing around without a job to do.'

'Yes, Doctor.' Maryanne snapped to it.

'Jasper, you take treatment room one, I'll go into two. We'll work from there. Now, if we could take a look at the reports which are coming in, please?' She held out her hand for the papers and was in the middle of scanning the third one when the wail of the sirens could be heard getting closer.

'Action stations,' she murmured.

'What did you say?' Jasper asked, a smirk on his face.

'Nothing.'

'Yes, you did. You said, "Action stations." '

'Perhaps I did.' She put the piece of paper from she'd been reading back onto the desk, then turned to look at him, lifting her chin slightly, the action causing Jasper's smile to increase. It wasn't the first time he'd seen her do that and he'd realised it was usually when she was uncomfortable. It was cute. 'What?' she asked when he continued to look at her, making her feel highly self-conscious.

He shrugged a little and stood from where he'd perched himself against the nurses' desk. 'Nothing. I guess it's just not something I'd expect you to say.'

'Why, not?' she asked as they both headed over towards the treatment cubicles.

'Well it's sort of . . . I don't know . . . a military expression.'

'And you don't see any resemblance between the military and a hospital?' she quizzed.

Jasper chuckled. 'I'm not denying that. I was just surprised to hear the words come out of your mouth. That's all.' He looked down at her as though excited about a new discovery. 'I like that about you. You're so different from other women.' With that, he headed into treatment room one whilst she went to number two.

While she pulled on a protective gown and gloves, Jennifer couldn't believe how warm his words made her feel. It had been an extremely long time since any man had said such sweet things to her and it was wonderful. Although, she rationalised, he was around females a lot, not only here at work with colleagues but at home with his daughters. He was obviously a father who was used to giving little compliments, to stroking the fragile female ego, and she'd probably do well not to put too much weight on what he said.

She'd come back to Parramatta hoping to find healing, to find the *real* Jennifer again, and accepting Jasper's easy banter and teasing was a good start. He had the ability to make her feel the way she had back in medical school before the weight of the world had been thrust on her shoulders. Arturo's death had affected her life because when he'd died she'd felt as though all of the life had gone out of her as well. If it hadn't been for close friends, such as Sara and Matt, she might have faded away into nothingness. Thankfully, though, she'd held on and now, coming back to Parramatta, back to where it had all begun, she was really starting to feel like her old self . . . willing to get out there and try to find her life once again. And Jasper was helping her.

Her first patient was wheeled in and she pushed all thoughts of Jasper to the back of her mind. The hours ticked by and after she'd seen one patient, ordered tests and X-rays, she moved on to the next. Apparently a truck had lost its brakes coming down an embankment on the freeway, and had not only collected the cars in front of it but also a few on the other side of the multiple-lane highway. Several cases had been transferred to Sydney General Hospital but as the accident had happened closer to Parramatta, their hospital would be responsible for the most urgent cases.

Eight hours later, just after midnight, Jennifer received a phone call as she was suturing a wound after inserting a nail that would stabilise the patient's femur.

'Dr Thorngate,' the scout nurse said. 'I have Eddie on the line. He says if you're free, could you meet him in Emergency Theatre Two, please? He needs your assistance.'

'Right. Thanks. Tell him I'll be there in ten minutes.' Jennifer looked across at Maryanne. 'You can close here, then you may as well grab a quick drink and check the status of future patients who may require our services tonight.'

'Yes, Dr Thorngate.'

Jennifer stood back from the table and put the instruments down, leaving the theatre staff to carry on while she pulled some extra energy from her already depleted reserves and went to assist Jasper.

When she entered Theatre Two, Jasper looked up from the table.

'Where have you been? I was told you'd be here in ten minutes.'

Jennifer's eyes widened at his tone and she quickly glanced at the clock. 'It's only been ten minutes.'

'It's been thirteen.'

She headed over, realising that if he was quibbling over a few minutes things probably weren't going too well. 'What do you need me to do?'

'Hold this retractor,' he ordered. The patient was a large man, covered in tattoos, and from what she could recall from when he'd been brought in had suffered a comminuted fracture of the right femur and fractures to the scapula and humerus. The pelvis, according to the X-rays that were up on the viewing box, showed a dislocation to the right acetabulum and an undisplaced fracture of the left acetabulum.

'I thought you were going to wait to deal with the pelvis in a few days' time, when the fracture had had time to settle a bit.'

'Oh, everyone's a critic.' Jasper's tone was heavy with fatigue and sarcasm.

'I was simply making a comment, Jasper.'

'No. You were criticising. Suction.'

'Hardly, but if that's the way you want to take my comments, don't let me stop you.'

'I won't.'

'Well, in that case, do you mind telling me what you're doing? This sort of fracture is best left for a few days or sometimes even a week.'

'This is you not criticising?' He glanced up at her and Jennifer saw that his earlier fatigue had been replaced by veiled humour. It was then she realised he needed to debate, to discuss, to enliven his mind through the fatigue, and that what he was saying wasn't what he really meant. It wasn't the first time she'd come across this sort of method to help the surgeon to stay alert. Personally, she preferred to have music on in her theatre, and not the soothing strains of classical music like most of her peers preferred. She was a rock 'n' roll girl.

'Yes, it is,' she retorted, lifting her chin in the way that he liked. Ah, she was quite a woman. 'Are you going to make something of it?'

He could see in her eyes that she understood what was happening, that she knew she was helping him to relax, and he thoroughly appreciated her efforts. 'I might,' he said, then chuckled. It was a good moment. The atmosphere when she'd walked in had been so taut she could have cut it with a scalpel, but now that Jasper had released his own tension, everybody else seemed to relax a little more, making it easier to concentrate.

'However, I'd like to state for the record that I hadn't planned to deal with the pelvis right now but I had no choice. I need to pin this section to increase stability. I'll revisit it in about a week's time.'

'Fair enough. Retract further,' she said to the nurse. 'Angle the light a little to the right, please.' Jennifer took a good look. 'Can we have some music on?'

'Eddie doesn't like to work to music,' Theatre Sister remarked crisply.

'What do you like listening to?' Jasper asked. 'Strauss? No, I know. How about Beethoven? His "1812 Overture" would be enough to wake the patient up, let alone keep the surgeon alert.'

'Well, I don't think we want the patient regaining consciousness just yet, Jasper.'

'Good point. So what tickles your fancy? Er . . . I mean, as far as music goes,' he quickly added, and a few of the staff laughed. Her eyes met his across the operating table and the look they shared in one brief second was enough to let her know he didn't only mean music.

'I'm a rock 'n' roll girl.'

'Really? Dr Thorngate, *you* are full of surprises.' He looked over at the scout nurse. 'Do we have any rock 'n' roll for Dr Thorngate?'

'We do, Eddie. Dr Thorngate still has a CD here from yesterday.'

'But, Eddie?' Theatre Sister was taken aback by his request.

'It's in the patient's best interests.' His tone was calm yet clearly brooked no argument. 'Dr Thorngate needs to stay alert and awake so she can keep the rest of us in line.'

'Hmph.' Theatre Sister wasn't at all happy and a few minutes later the first few opening bars of 'Johnny B. Goode' came through the speakers.

They worked on, stabilising their patient's fracture before Jasper did a final check and announced himself satisfied. He left Allan to close the wound and headed out with Jennifer, both of them degowning.

'Is there more?' Jasper slumped into a chair. 'Please say the answer is no.'

'I'm not sure.' She walked over to the phone on the wall and called through to the nurses' station. 'Is Maryanne there?'

'Yes. I'll put her on,' the nurse said. While Jennifer waited, she looked over at Jasper who had his hands laced behind his head and his eyes closed. He was stretched out across the chair, his long legs crossed at the ankles, but the way he was lounging made the top of his scrub shirt rise up and his scrub trousers dip down. Her eyes were automatically drawn to the firm muscles of his lower abdomen and she realised that although she liked his firm arms and broad shoulders, the rest of him seemed to be just as fine. Nice. *Very* nice.

Jennifer turned her head, averting her eyes as she spoke to the registrar on the phone, but Jasper couldn't believe she'd just given him a thorough once-over. It had been brief yet breathtaking; careful yet caressing, sweet yet sensual. She may have given him a quick appraisal earlier, when they'd been teasing Sara, but this had been real. Desire had flared in her eyes and it was obvious that she liked what she saw. As far as he was concerned, it had been a long time since any woman, sneaking a glance at him, had made him feel as though he were a teenager again, but that was how he felt.

He watched Jennifer as she quickly reached for a piece of paper and pen and scribbled some notes down. Even in baggy theatre scrubs, she looked good. Her hair was still pulled back into that bun, the style she'd worn day in, day out, and while it might be practical, especially when they were in Theatre, he was becoming more than curious to find out what she looked like with those dark locks of hers flowing free and lovely.

When she hung up, he sat up straighter in his chair. 'What's the verdict?'

'Theatre One. Patient requiring open reduction and internal fixation of three fractured limbs.'

'Really?' he groaned, his body heavy with fatigue.

'I'll take it.'

'No, it's all right. I can do it.'

'Seriously, Jasper, it's fine.'

'It's all right,' he repeated, meeting her gaze. 'Can't have the new boss thinking I'm a wimp.'

Jennifer smiled. 'Hardly.' She held out a fist towards him. 'I'll play you for it.'

'Pardon?'

'Rock, paper, scissors?'

He blinked, doing a double-take. Was she serious? First he discovered she liked rock 'n' roll when she operated and now she was making a decision about who was going to do an operation by using the rock, paper, scissors method. She was . . . enigmatic.

'Is there anything else urgent that needs doing?'

'Just triage cases.'

He thought for a moment then nodded. 'The registrars can handle those.' He stood and held his hand out palm up. 'Paper. Paper wraps rock.'

'Hey, we hadn't started,' she complained, but stopped short as Jasper actually wrapped his hand around her fist. The touch was enough to ignite the flame that had been on a slow burn for the past two weeks.

Jasper looked into her eyes, not removing his hand. 'Why don't we both do it? We'll get through it faster.'

'Uh . . . actually . . .' Jennifer sucked in a breath. His hand was warm and comfortable and she liked it far too much. She swallowed and cleared her throat. 'Why don't you head home? I can deal with it. Shouldn't be too much longer and, well, you know, I have my music to keep me company. Go home and get some sleep. The girls will no doubt wake up bright and early tomorrow.'

'It's fine,' he said, leaning in a little. It was as though he could see her reaction to his nearness and he wanted to prolong it. 'The girls are asleep and I'm more than used to being woken up bright and early after only a few hours' sleep.'

His eyes were becoming intense now and Jennifer knew she wasn't strong enough to handle it. It was as though this thing between them was slowly increasing in intensity. Something that was more than either being colleagues or friends. She wasn't sure what it was and she didn't know if she wanted to find out.

Edging back, she removed her hand from his touch and took a few steps away, needing distance. Her mind searched for something to say but for a few seconds it appeared to be blank. Thankfully, she recalled what he'd just said and almost pounced on it.

'Come to think of it, where *are* your girls? I mean, you're here at work. Do they have a day-care lady or a friend who looks after them at night?'

'They're with my parents.'

'Oh, of course. I forgot your parents usually look after them. Sara did mention that. So, do your parents live close?'

Jasper thought of them living on the first floor of his house. 'Uh . . . you could say that.'

'So the girls have a room at their house and just sleep over when necessary?'

He shrugged nonchalantly. 'Something like that.'

'Jasper, you're being coy.'

'Coy?' He laughed at that. 'Men aren't *coy*. Only women are coy. I'm being . . . deliberately evasive.' He shook his head and chuckled. 'Coy. What a word. You do make me laugh, Jennifer.'

'I think that's a compliment.'

'It is.' His tone and his look were equally as expressive. He stared at her for a moment, as though not sure what to say next.

'Oh.' Jennifer wasn't used to getting such direct compliments. In fact, she wasn't used to getting compliments, full stop.

'And if you *must* know,' he continued, 'my parents live with us.'

'You still live at home?' She was surprised at that, her lips twitching with amusement.

'No. No,' he said firmly. 'I said my parents live with us. There's a difference.' He looked around them but there was no one else about. 'I'll have you know that I moved out of home a long time ago. I bought my own house, got married, had a couple of kids, then when Elisha died, I remodelled the house so that my parents could sell their big rambling home and move in. It's an arrangement that works well for everyone, especially the girls.'

'Fair enough.' She was touched that he'd explained because it showed her he really was willing to cross that line between the professional world and the personal one they were both so desperate to keep separate. Jennifer knew she'd been crossing the line more often than not of late and to know he was willing to do it too made her feel a little more comfortable.

'So are we going to get this next patient done so we can both go home?'

'I guess so but honestly, Jasper, you can go now and —'

'Paper beats rock.' He took her hand in his, wrapping his fingers loosely around hers again, watching the way her eyes flared with a spark of excitement before it was quickly veiled. 'Remember?'

Jennifer's breath caught in her throat not only at his touch but at the look in his eyes. It was deep, rich and seriously intimate. Where his touch had been mildly playful before, this time it was as sensual as if he'd brushed a thumb across her lips. His body was close to hers, closer than before, and as her heart rate increased, she found it was becoming increasingly difficult to breathe.

'Jasper?' His name was a confused caress on her lips and as his eyes dipped to take in the lush fullness of her mouth, her breath caught in her throat. 'Don't look at me like that,' she whispered hoarsely.

'Why not?'

'Because you make me sizzle and I don't know how to deal with that.'

'Sizzle?' His resolve to keep things light, to keep on ignoring the enormous tug he continually felt towards her, was beginning to crack. He'd felt the tug of something new and exciting between them since the first moment they'd met — even before they'd discovered their external connection — and he'd worked extremely hard to ignore it. So, it seemed, had Jennifer. When she said things like that, it was enough to make his logical thought processes shut down and instinct take over — and his instinctive reaction was to press his mouth firmly to hers and show her what it would really feel like to sizzle.

The phone on the wall rang and both of them sprang apart, startled and jumpy. They stared at the inanimate object for a moment before Jasper snatched it up. 'Eddie,' he said into the receiver.

It was the distraction Jennifer needed and she quickly walked from the room, heading to Theatre One, hoping Jasper would change his mind and decide not to join her because right now she wasn't sure she could deal with him being so close when she was supposed to be concentrating on a patient.

Never before had she had this problem. Never had she been unable to focus her mind on her work, as she'd experienced a few times thanks to Jasper Edwards and his overwhelming, enigmatic presence.

She'd scrubbed and had just started working when he entered the room. Again she felt him before she saw him and was surprised at her own intuitiveness where he was concerned. She found it difficult to meet his eyes and so simply kept her gaze down and on the job, wanting to get this night over and done with so she could sneak quietly into Sara's house, wrap herself up in her blankets and just disappear.

Thankfully, at some time during the two hours they spent working on their patient, Jennifer began to relax and realised that as there was currently nothing she could do about the obvious attraction she felt towards her handsome colleague, she'd do well to simply push it aside.

'Finally!' Jasper pulled off his gloves, mask and gown, putting them in the appropriate bins and heading out of Theatre with Jennifer not far behind him. 'Have we beaten the sunrise?' he wanted to know as they walked towards the changing rooms.

'Uh . . . I think we might have but not by much.'

Jasper stopped outside the door marked MALE and looked at her. 'Listen, Jennifer, I know this is no doubt against the unwritten rules we seem to have made and I don't want you to feel pressured at all but . . . would you like to come over for breakfast?'

'Over?'

'To my house.'

'House?' Her brain seemed incapable of rational thought and it didn't help at all when his lips started tugging upwards.

'Sure. We've both been up all night long and could do with some breakfast.'

'Breakfast?'

Jasper's lips beamed into a full-blown smile and she wished they hadn't. 'Yes. Obviously spending a busy night in and out of Theatre affects your powers of speech — or at least the power of forming sentences. Breakfast. The meal you eat at the beginning of the day?'

'Hmm.' She nodded slowly, still totally mesmerised by his smile.

'Anyway, the girls would like to see you and after breakfast we could wander down and see if Mr Attenburgh is happy for you to see the house.'

'Oh!' Jennifer covered her mouth with her hand. 'The house! I'd totally forgotten about the house and my appointment.'

'I didn't. I called him before going into my first theatre case and told him we'd reschedule.'

'Thanks.' She sighed, unable to believe she'd forgotten. She'd tried several times in the past fortnight to view the house but various obstacles and problems had kept delaying her. Now she simply wanted to get it over and done with. If it was as perfect as Jasper seemed to think, hopefully she'd be able to settle and move in quickly.

But first things first. Jasper had asked her over to his house for breakfast. Her first reaction was to accept instantly but her second was to weigh up the pros and cons. His nearness was starting to do things to her she wasn't sure she could control in such a personal and comfortable setting and that in itself was scary enough. Control had been her close friend for many years but it was also sort of exciting to have that little bit of spontaneity in her life. Besides, not only would she have the opportunity to see over the house and get that crossed off her list but she'd get to see Jasper's girls again. She'd enjoyed playing with them when they'd been at Sara's house and she had to admit she was becoming more curious about Jasper Edwards — the man, not the surgeon.

Jasper could see her internal struggle. 'I'll make you pancakes,' he offered temptingly.

Her eyes glazed over for a moment, then he saw the beginnings of a small smile. 'Really?'

'I make them light and fluffy.' He almost had her. He was reeling her in and he was loving every moment of it.

'They're my favourite.'

'There you go, then. I'll even do bacon and eggs to give breakfast a bit more of a . . . sizzle.' He waggled his eyebrows up and down as he spoke and Jennifer looked away, surprised when she felt her cheeks suffuse with colour.

'Don't, Jasper.' Her words were barely audible but he heard.

'Don't what?'

'Tease. I . . . I didn't mean to say that.'

'What? That I make you sizzle?'

'Stop it.' Even his words, the way he was looking at her now made her start to sizzle once more. If she was totally honest with herself, she would accept that she wanted to spend more and more time with him and she wanted to do that as far away from her life at the hospital.

'Why?' Jasper checked the corridor, pleased to find it still deserted. He reached out and placed his hand lightly on her shoulder. When he spoke, his tone was soft, intimate. 'You're the first woman who's ever said that to me. That I make her sizzle. I liked it.'

When she didn't say anything else, he gave her shoulder a little squeeze before dropping his hand. 'It's just breakfast, Jen. The girls will be there, so will my parents. It's not as though it's a date or anything. Think of it more as eating food together in a non-hospital environment.'

'Like the other night?'

'Exactly.'

He was right. She was over-thinking things again, something she'd promised herself she'd try not to do. She wanted to have breakfast with him, she wanted to see his girls again and she wanted to take a look at the house. Spending all of that time with Jasper would be an added bonus . . . and to top it all off he'd called her Jen. Wasn't that the first sign of acceptance? The move from colleagues to good friends?

Her smile was small but her eyes sparkled with interest. 'OK.'

'Excellent.' With a matching smile, he turned and entered the change rooms, leaving her feeling as though she'd just taken a very important step towards living. *Really* living.

CHAPTER FOUR

'Daddy! Daddy!' Both girls hurled themselves at the door the instant they heard it open, and within a moment Jasper had an identical twin wrapped around each leg. He laughed as he dropped his briefcase and bent down to scoop them up, one on each side. Jennifer couldn't believe the absolute delight on his face, especially when they put their arms around his neck and began kissing his cheeks — again, the attack was performed with perfect synchronicity.

'Hello, my monkeys.' Jasper kissed them both, one then the other and back again for a repeat.

'We're not monkeys,' one said, blonde ringlets bobbing from side to side as she wriggled in her father's arms.

'We're princesses,' the other replied, then rolled her eyes at her sister. 'He always gets it wrong.'

Jasper bent to put them down and it was

then Lilly, or maybe it was Lola — Jennifer was having a difficult time telling them apart, especially in their matching pink princess pyjamas — looked over and saw her.

'Jen.' She stood there with her little hands on her little hips and angled her head to the side, a ringlet springing up and down. 'What are you doing here? You're s'pposed to be at Sara's house.'

'Jen? Why aren't you at Sara's?' the other one said, mimicking her sister's pose.

'Hello, girls.' Jennifer smiled at both of them. 'Jas— er . . . Daddy invited me over to have breakfast with you.' Jennifer licked her lips and rubbed her tummy with exaggeration. 'He told me he'd make pancakes and they're my favourite.'

'Mine, too.'

'Yeah. Mine, too,' repeated the other twin.

'I'm gonna tell Grandma.'

'No. *I'm* gonna tell Grandma.' With that, the two of them raced off towards the stairs and a moment later footsteps could be heard above them as they ran through the upper floor.

'Sorry.' Jasper shed his coat then picked up his briefcase from just inside the door where he'd quickly put it down before being bombarded by his daughters.

'What for?'

'Uh-h . . .' He stopped for a moment and looked at her. 'You know? I'm not sure.'

Jennifer smiled at him, liking the way he looked in these surroundings, liking the way he looked when he looked at her with twinkling, shining eyes. She turned away, indicating the living room which contained a wall-to-wall bookshelf, a large television and DVD player, two comfortable sofas and lots of big, bright throw pillows on the floor. On two of the walls were various pieces of abstract art which no doubt the girls had done at pre-school.

'I like the way you've decorated.' It was then she remembered that he'd mentioned his wife had decorated their bedroom. Had she done this room, too?

Jasper turned and looked at the room, then laughed. 'Lots of . . . colour.'

'That's what children do, isn't it? They fill your world with colour.'

'And a lot of other things along the way.' He picked up two soft toys that had been left on the floor as he walked through an archway. 'Come through. Let me take your coat.' He threw the toys onto a nearby chair then quickly hung up his own coat before helping her off with her own. Jennifer was conscious of his nearness, his warm, earthy

98

scent surrounding her and making her very aware of him. 'You can either sit at the table or keep me company at the bench while I cook.'

He hung up her coat, then headed into the kitchen, his voice a little deeper than before. He cleared his throat to try and make it sound more normal. Jennifer's perfume had wound its way about his senses and for a split second he'd found himself unable to move as he'd helped her out of her coat. There was definitely an awareness between them . . . or at least that's the way he was reading the situation. The woman was stunningly beautiful and intelligent and although he knew she was fresh from a shower, as was he, whatever it was that she wore would continue to drive him crazy long after she'd left.

As he entered the kitchen, he was glad he'd spent the few extra minutes cleaning up before heading to work the previous morning. The bench was wiped, the dishwasher cycle was finished and the stove was ready for him to cook on. It would have been embarrassing to bring home a woman — for the very first time — to a messy kitchen.

'Coffee?' he asked.

'Actually, a cup of tea would be lovely.'

'Tea coming right up.' He filled the kettle then switched it on.

'So do you make pancakes most mornings? I'm only asking because the girls seemed overly excited at the prospect.'

'Usually only on weekends. I think their overexcitedness pertains to having someone over to share it with them.'

'Oh. That's nice. So why did they need to go and tell your mother they were having pancakes?'

Jasper's eyes twinkled as he spoke. 'They'll be telling her about you, not the food.'

'Oh,' she said again, not sure what to make of this news. He didn't seem to mind so she could only presume he was all too happy to introduce her to his parents. Was that good? Did that mean things were moving way too fast? Or was it simply a fact that she would meet his parents sooner or later, given their connection through Sara? 'Is that a problem?'

'Not at all.' He brushed her worries aside. If he told her he'd never brought a woman into his home, into his life, she might start to feel even more self-conscious than she already was. 'Now, as pancakes are your favourite food, I'm expecting an open and honest assessment of my secret recipe.'

'Secret, huh? Very intriguing.'

He leaned a little closer, then looked first one way then the other, as though he was about to impart the greatest secret in the world. 'I use buttermilk.' He straightened, then shrugged. 'Not so secret but, oh, so light and fluffy.'

Jennifer licked her lips. 'I can hardly wait.'

'But wait you shall. It'll be easier if I feed the girls first.'

'Of course. That's the one problem with making pancakes at home — unless you have a big griddle plate, you basically can only make one at a time.'

'You make them often?'

Jennifer shrugged. 'When I was living in Melbourne, I did. It's been a bit hard at Sara's to just whip up a batch at two o'clock in the morning when I've finished wading through my mound of inherited paperwork.'

Jasper laughed. 'I'm so glad the paperwork is your headache now and not mine.' As he spoke, they could hear footsteps coming down the stairs.

'Heads up.' His words were soft as he continued to pull out the utensils and ingredients for pancakes as well as the eggs and bacon.

'Good morning, Jasper.' His mother's calm tones greeted him as she came in to the room. Jasper's mother was no taller than

Jennifer, had short grey hair and sparkling blue eyes, big and vibrant, like those of her granddaughters.

'See!' Lilly remarked.

'We *told* you Jen was here.'

'So you did,' their grandmother replied, and held out her hand, not waiting for Jasper to introduce them. 'Hello. I'm Iris.'

'Jennifer.' The two women shook hands. 'I'm happy to meet you. I've heard a lot about you.'

Iris arched an eyebrow in her son's direction but Jasper shook his head. 'Not from me, Mum.'

Jennifer smiled warmly. 'I'm a friend of Sara's. I've been staying with her for the past few weeks so I've seen the girls there a few times.'

'Oh.' Iris came and sat down beside her. 'That's what the girls were talking about. They said that Sara's friend was here but that their daddy had brought someone home for pancakes. I was getting confused so I thought I'd come and see what they were on about.'

'As it turns out,' Jasper said, whisking the mixture, 'Jennifer is my new boss.'

'You *work* together?' Iris was stunned as she looked pointedly at her son and then back at Jennifer.

'Yes.' Jennifer was working hard at not squirming — and she wasn't doing too badly, if she did say so herself. She'd been scrutinised from all angles before, given her job in medical administration, yet she hadn't been looked at this closely by a man's mother before. 'Is there something wrong?'

'Remember how I said I like to keep my private and professional lives separate?' Jasper reminded her as he put the first pancake on to cook. He spoke in a quieter voice but knew full well his mother could hear him.

'Ah.' Jennifer clicked then as to why his mother was astonished. 'I take it you usually don't invite colleagues home for breakfast after a gruelling night in theatre?'

'No. Mum, Jennifer's looking to buy a house,' Jasper added before his mother could say anything more. 'We're going to have some breakfast, then go and see Mr Attenburgh.'

'The house down the road?'

'Is there another one in the street for sale?' Jasper asked pointedly.

The phone rang and the girls, who hadn't been very interested in the adult conversation up until now, immediately shouted, 'I'll get it.'

'No. *I'll* get it,' one said. 'It's my turn.'

'No, it's *my* turn.' They both started jostling each other out of the way as they raced from the room towards the phone.

'How about if I get it,' Jasper said, and stalked after them, shaking his head. 'At least that will stop World War Three,' he muttered, and Jennifer couldn't help but smile.

'They argue over who should answer the phone every time it rings at Sara's place,' Jennifer pointed out as Iris still stared at her. When the woman didn't stop, Jennifer shifted in her seat, beginning to feel rather uncomfortable. 'Is something wrong?' she couldn't help but ask again.

'Wrong?' Iris pulled back as though she wasn't aware she'd been staring. 'No. Nothing is wrong. So, you work . . . closely with Jasper?'

'We're both the only orthopods employed full time by the hospital so I guess you could say that. He's been great at helping me get settled in.'

'And you've just been in Theatre all night long, right?'

'Pretty much. Bad motor vehicle accidents. Lots of casualties.'

'And you've obviously met the girls before now. They appear quite comfortable with you.'

'They do?'

'Oh, yes. Usually when they meet a new friend of their father's . . . If they ever get to meet them, of course, they normally hide behind his legs until they get to know them better. Naturally, though, they don't get to know them better because Jasper's far too fussy.'

'Fussy?' Jennifer wasn't quite sure she was on the same track as Iris but decided to go with it.

'When he dates!' Iris seemed surprised that Jennifer wasn't sure what she was talking about. 'He doesn't introduce his dates to the girls, which is fair enough because he wants to protect them as any father would, and I'm in complete agreement, but you'd think that after a few times of seeing the same woman he'd eventually introduce them, but no.'

'Jasper's dating someone?' Jennifer wasn't quite sure why the news made her feel instantly miserable.

'No, no.' Iris waved her words away. 'I'm talking about in the past but now here you are, as plain as day, invited over for breakfast, and he's only been working with you for a few weeks.'

Jennifer wasn't sure what that meant but as Jasper came back in to the room she had no time to contemplate it further.

'Was that the hospital?'

'No. It was Megan.'

'Oh?' Iris was instantly concerned.

'Megan's my sister,' Jasper informed Jennifer.

'Is everything all right?' Iris was on her feet, getting ready to head for the stairs. 'Why is she calling you and why so early?'

'Relax, Mum. She was just ringing to see if the girls' dresses had arrived yet.'

'And have they?'

'No.'

Iris shook her head and took another step towards the stairs. 'I'd best go call her. She'll be fretting over that.' Iris started off then stopped and turned to Jennifer. 'It was really nice to meet you.'

'And you, too.' As Iris left, Jennifer turned to watch Jasper flipping the first pancake. 'You're quite good at that.'

'One of my many talents. I'm thinking of adding it to my résumé.'

She smiled at that. 'I'd certainly hire you.' She paused then asked, 'Why is your mother so concerned about your sister?'

'Megan's getting married in three weeks' time. Lilly and Lola are her flower girls.'

'And the dresses haven't arrived.' Jennifer nodded as though everything now made perfect sense. 'That should be enough to make a bride go completely berserk.'

'You've got that right and Megan's stress levels are already at an all-time high.' He frowned a little. 'Problem is, Mum and Dad don't approve of her husband-to-be. He hasn't done anything to help plan the wedding, not that that's totally unusual but whenever Megan's asked him, he's flatly refused. It's made things more burdensome for her. Add to that fact that she's due in Theatre in another hour and she's one mega-stressed puppy.'

'Theatre?'

'She's a general surgeon over at Sydney General.'

'Hmm. Quite the medical family.'

Jasper smiled and flipped another pancake. 'She's incredibly smart. I was two years ahead of her in medical school but she was the one helping me out and explaining things.'

Jennifer laughed. 'Should you be confessing such things to your new boss?'

'Not to worry.' He set two butterfly placemats on the bench next to her and added cutlery before cutting up the pancakes into little squares. He did it all so naturally she could tell it was part of his routine. He was clearly a dad who spent a lot of time with his children. 'I passed my exams with flying colours and haven't had to rely on my baby sister for quite a number of years.' He called to the girls, who came barrelling in and clambered up onto stools. Lilly managed it quite easily but Lola got stuck and Jennifer quickly picked her up and sat her down before Jasper could come around to help.

'Thanks,' he said.

'No problem.' She smiled at him as he added syrup to the girls' breakfasts and watched as they devoured the food in next to no time. 'You must have been very hungry,' Jennifer commented.

Lilly nodded enthusiastically. 'I was.'

'Anyone would think your daddy rarely feeds you.'

'We had dinner at Grandma's last night 'cause Daddy was in surgery,' Lola added matter-of-factly.

'We do that. Sometimes we have breakfast at Grandma's, too,' Lilly chimed in.

'But it's just up the stairs,' Lola pointed.

'Not too far,' Lilly agreed.

'Now, my yummy princesses,' Jasper said as he added another pancake to the warming plate he had in the oven, 'time for a bath.' His words were received with mild protests. 'You're both covered in syrup,' he pointed out when they asked why.

'But, Daddy, why can't you just wipe us down with the cloth? Then we will be all ready to play.'

'Planning to wear your jimmy-jams all day long?' He smiled at Jennifer before excusing himself to go and run the bath. Jennifer sat there, looking around his home, and was surprised to find it very welcoming. Usually when she went to a new friend's house, it took quite some time for her to feel comfortable but, like at Sara's house, she felt quite relaxed here.

Jennifer looked at the pancake he'd put on the stove to cook before he'd gone off to tend to his daughters and quickly went to check on it. He'd turned the heating element down so it was cooking at a slower rate but now that she was up, she decided to at least make herself useful. After checking on the sizzling bacon and eggs, she checked the dishwasher and found it full but clean. Quietly and quickly, she took the dishes out, and after opening a few cupboards, was able to figure out where most things went. Next, she put the girls' sticky plates and cutlery into the dishwasher then wiped down their placemats and the bench. It was quite nice to potter around in his kitchen . . . a kitchen that serviced a real family. It brought home to her how her own little kitchen at her flat in Melbourne in retrospect seemed bare and lifeless as she'd prepared meals for one.

She'd flipped the pancake and was about to take it out and pour another when Jasper came rushing back.

'Oh, thanks, Jennifer. I hadn't planned to be that long. Lola has syrup in her hair so I'll need to wash it but first, let's have some breakfast in peace while the girls get themselves and the bathroom nice and wet.'

Jennifer laughed and moved aside so Jasper could return to the stove. She decided to help a bit further and took out plates and cutlery for the two of them, then reboiled the kettle, found two cups and put them on the bench.

'Here you go.' Jasper handed her the teabags, amazed at the warming sensation he was experiencing at having a woman poking about in his kitchen. He been so used to being chief cook and bottlewasher for years that it was nice to be sharing it with someone else, even if it was just a one-off thing.

When it came time to eat the two stacks of pancakes Jasper put before her, Jennifer couldn't help exclaiming at the taste. 'These are heavenly. So light. So fluffy.'

'As you're a connoisseur of pancakes, I'll take that as a very high compliment.'

'Mmm. You should. Delicious.' When she'd finished, she licked her lips. He watched the action intently, not surprised to experience a mild tightening in his gut. He'd never thought he would be jealous of a pancake. He was enjoying this time alone with her . . . just the two of them . . . and even though he could hear the girls in the distance, squealing and laughing, it didn't matter one bit. He was here, in his house, alone with Jennifer.

'More?' he offered, and watched as she eyed the fresh pancake still in the pan. 'Go on.'

'OK. You've talked me into it.'

'Wasn't difficult.' He scooped it out and put it on her plate, secretly pleased that she liked his cooking.

'How did you make them again?'

'You were sitting right in front of me when I did it,' he pointed out.

'Yes, but I was distracted not only by your daughters but by your mother's inquisitive stare.'

'She was staring?' Jasper was horrified and closed his eyes for a moment, shaking his head. 'I'm so sorry, Jennifer.'

She laughed. 'Don't apologise. She was just surprised, I guess, that you'd brought a colleague home.'

'It has nothing to do with you being a colleague, Jennifer, let me tell you that right now. It does, however, have everything to do with you being a woman.'

'Oh. You don't bring your dates home for pancakes?' As she said the words, she realised that they could be taken another way. 'Er . . . I mean . . .'

Jasper laughed, watching the way a small flush of colour tinged her cheeks. She was becoming more adorable, more addictive with each passing moment. 'I know what you meant and the answer is no. I haven't brought the *few* women I've dated home to have breakfast with me and my family. You're the first.'

'But I'm not your date.'

'No, but definitely the first woman.' He stood and cleared the plates, switching the kettle on again for another cuppa, knowing he needed to keep things light. 'It's as you've said, though. We both know Sara. We'll both be mixing socially, as well as working together at the hospital, so even though we may not have mixed those worlds in the past, they'll definitely be mixing in the future.'

'So I take it from what your mother said that the girls have never met anyone you've dated?'

'Nope. They don't need short-term acquaintances coming in and out of their lives. Way too confusing for them and far too many questions for me to answer.'

'Ah, now we come to the real crux of the matter. You're scared of your girls.'

'Scared of the way they'd question me to death? Yes.'

'I take it you don't classify me as a short-term acquaintance?'

Jasper thought about that for a moment. 'No. Your work contract is for at least the next two years but as you're now in your dream job, I doubt you'll be giving it up after that. Add to all of that the fact that you already know the girls, which makes you a low-risk friend.'

'Low risk?'

'Low risk of hurting them.' And me, he added silently. Inviting Jennifer home had been done on a whim and he wasn't the type of man to give in to whims, especially where the girls were concerned. He might even tell himself that he'd only done it so he could help Jennifer see the house down the street, as he would have done for any other colleague, but deep down he knew he'd wanted to see how Jennifer looked in his world and he had to admit she looked pretty darn good.

Their eyes met and held, both of them content to simply stand there for a moment and connect. Jennifer wasn't at all sure how this happened but it was as though she could *feel* whatever Jasper was thinking about. It was a connection on a level she hadn't really encountered before, not even with Arturo. In one way she was delighted to be experiencing something new, but on the other hand it terrified her. She wasn't good at taking steps outside her comfort zone. Still, Jasper looked at her, the colour of his irises deepening with an appreciation for the woman before him. She could see it. Could see the attraction he'd spoken of the other night when they'd had dinner. They hadn't known each other long but it was as though they'd known each other for ever. It was as though both were too scared to take that first giant leap of exploration yet eager to get the expedition started.

'Strange.' The word was barely audible as it slipped through her lips and Jasper's gaze dipped to her mouth as though he was eager to explore that terrain as well. He moved, taking a step closer, needing to close the distance between them but maintaining eye contact at all times.

The giggling and splashing from the bathroom became louder and Jasper eased back, rolling his eyes. 'Never a dull moment.'

'Go and deal with them and I'll tidy the kitchen.' Distance. She needed distance, if for nothing else than to pull herself together.

He was about to refuse her offer of help but decided against it. Nodding, he agreed. 'OK. Thanks.' He headed off in the direction of the bathroom and Jennifer smiled as she heard him questioning his daughters, wanting to know why the bathroom floor was covered with water. Not too much later, she laughed as one of the girls came streaking past stark naked, with Jasper hot on her heels, before he scooped her up and carried her back to her room.

Jennifer relaxed and made herself another cup of tea, pushing down the yearning she could feel beginning to rise. She'd wanted a life like this. A family of her own. She *should* have had one by now and if things had gone to plan, the children she and Art had been planning to have should have been around seven years old by now. Jennifer shook her head. Her life would have been very different.

'But you wouldn't have been head of unit at such a young age — *if* you could call thirty-eight young,' she whispered softly to herself. Still, the words didn't seem to matter much when faced with what her alternative life would have been like.

By half past seven, the girls were freshly washed and dressed ready for the day ahead. Jasper had called Mr Attenburgh to make sure it was all right to come down and then announced to both girls they were going for a little walk.

'Is it all right to go this early?' Jennifer checked as the girls went to get their coats as it was definitely a chilly July morning.

'Oh, Mr Attenburgh goes for a walk at a quarter to six every morning. He's awake, alive, alert and enthusiastic.'

'Good to hear.'

'Lilly? Are you staying here with Grandma?' he asked when she didn't come back with her coat. 'You don't have to come, honey.'

'I'll stay and look after Grandma.' Lilly was already on the stairs. 'Lola will look after you and Jen, Daddy.'

'Good to see they're already looking out for their dad,' Jennifer remarked as the three of them headed outside into the crisp morning, tucking her scarf more firmly into the top of her coat.

'Lilly is the nurturer. Lola is the adventurer,' he said as Lola positioned herself between the two of them, slipping her hands into theirs and then asking for a swing.

'I love swings. Lilly doesn't,' Lola added. 'But I do. *A lot.*'

'What does she mean?' Jennifer asked.

'We count to three and then we lift her forward and up into the air.' Jasper counted and after three, up went Lola, giggling with glee. Again and again they did this with the child laughing each time.

'She doesn't get tired of it?'

'Nope. Do it to Lilly and she snaps your head off. Doesn't like the sensation that she's flying through the sky, our Lil.'

'Have you ever got them confused?' Jennifer was still trying to search for a way she might be able to tell them apart.

'Nope. Believe it or not, they look completely different to me.'

'Perhaps because you see them more as personalities rather than focusing on the physical appearance.'

'Hmm. I'd never thought of it like that before. You're probably right.'

They continued to swing Lola, who was laughing brightly in the crisp morning, providing her own brand of sweet sunshine. It was enough to warm Jennifer's heart and as she glanced over at Jasper the yearning deep inside her to have this sort of life for

117

her own, to have a husband and family of her own, was almost overwhelming.

CHAPTER FIVE

They gave Lola one last swing as they came to the house in question. Jennifer stopped and looked at the outside. It was a brick house, with a bay window at the front. She'd always loved bay windows and the house she'd bought with Art all those years ago had had three bay windows across the front.

'Jennifer?' Jasper called when she stopped stock still. Lola was busy trying to tug him down the driveway but Jasper had seen a strange look come into Jennifer's eyes. 'Do you like it?' he asked. Jennifer didn't answer. Instead, she simply stood there and he realised she was miles away. What was she thinking of? Her expression was one of wistful yearning and in that moment he knew she was probably thinking of her past. He knew that look because he'd worn it several times himself.

'Jennifer?' he tried again, and was successful in rousing her.

'Hmm? Sorry.' She snapped out of her reverie and turned to look at him.

'Do you like it?'

Jennifer sighed and nodded. 'I do. The front garden's small but I'm not looking for a big garden.' The arrangement of native trees and shrubs with their evergreen leaves made the small area look lush and inviting.

'The back yard is big enough to have a few friends around but small enough that it doesn't need a lot of upkeep.' He pointed with his free hand, Lola still tugging on the other one. 'Shall we go and see Mr Attenburgh before Lola does some real damage to my arm?'

She nodded. 'Good idea. I'm too tired to reset a dislocated humerus.'

Jennifer discovered the inside of the two-bedroomed house was as quaint and as lovely as the outside, and the bay window already had a window-seat just waiting for her to curl up and relax after a hard day at the hospital. The house was empty, all the furniture having been shifted as Mr Attenburgh already had his new residence.

'You could move in straight away,' the old man told her. 'Once the papers have been signed, of course,' he added with a full, dentured smile.

It suited her perfectly and she promised

to let him know soon. When they returned to Jasper's house, he sent Lola off to find Lilly then turned to Jennifer, eager to ask her opinion.

'You obviously liked the house.'

'Yes.' She sat down on the lounge, shifting slightly to face him as he sat next to her.

His eyes were clear yet unswerving. 'There's more to it than that, right?'

It was on the tip of her tongue to deny his words, to tell him to mind his own business, to freeze him out, but when she looked into those powerful grey eyes, which were so gentle yet highly intelligent, she realised Jasper Edwards was someone she could come to trust. He'd been through his own misery, his own grief and no doubt that was why he was picking up on her body language and out-of-synch emotions. 'Yes.'

'You teared up when you saw the window-seat.'

She thought he hadn't noticed. 'Yes.'

'Why?' The question was soft yet his curiosity about her was evident in his expression. It showed her he wanted to know more about her and she knew in getting to know someone better, that inevitably meant talking about the past. *Her* past.

'I like bay windows. I always have.' She sighed and shrugged when he didn't question her further. She knew he was waiting for more, waiting for the explanation he could no doubt sense was there. He was too clever and too sweet for her to evade any longer.

'My father was in the army and, as you might guess, that meant we moved quite a bit during my childhood. Usually, the houses we lived in were either on the army base or else provided for my father in a suburb close to his work. One of the houses we moved to when I was twelve had a bay window. It had curtains which you could close to make a little hiding hole, where the whole world would be locked out, and I would sit there and read or just think and imagine.'

Jasper watched as she spoke, watched the wistfulness on her face as well as hearing the veiled pain in her voice.

'My parents didn't have a happy marriage. My father was a very oppressive man and my mother was the epitome of a military wife. When I was twelve my father was forced to retire due to ill health. We moved from the bay-window house into the first home my parents had ever owned. In one way it was good because I was finally able to settle down and make real friends and complete my schooling in one place.'

'Where you met Sara?'

'Yes.'

'It couldn't have been easy for your father, being forced to retire so early.'

'No. It wasn't. He was almost fifty and had trouble settling into a world where barking orders at people didn't seem to work any more. Instead, he decided to turn to alcohol for support. Life . . . sort of changed after that.'

Something in her tone made Jasper wary. 'Did he hurt you?' Jennifer didn't answer, sitting still, staring into nothingness. He put his hand on hers, his gentle touch bringing her back to the present. His tone was urgent. He needed to know. 'Jennifer. Did he —'

'No.' She shook her head emphatically. 'He never hit us, never touched us.'

'Us? You have siblings?'

'No. I meant Mum and I.'

'Where are your parents now?'

'Darwin. We don't speak. Too much water under the bridge and all that. Enter Sara.' She pushed her natural smile through the pain. 'Sara came into my life and showed me what a real family was like. I spent a lot of time at her place and not once did her parents quibble about it. My mother only needed to know where I was. My father cared about nothing but himself and his depression.'

'And you and Sara have been friends since.'

'We have.' Jennifer looked down at where his hand lay on hers, amazed at how incredible it felt to have such a caring touch offered. It was what she'd missed the most. Not having that one special person there to confide in. Not having the simplest of touches to let you know that someone cared about you. The companionship. The friendship. The deep, abiding relationship. Was it possible she could find something resembling those missing parts of her life with Jasper? She took a deep breath and slowly let it out.

'And through my friendship with Sara . . .' Her words were soft and a little shaky but she persevered. 'You've come into my life.' She slowly lifted her eyes to his and when she was finally looking into his grey depths she saw an desperate need, a need which she knew was mirrored in her own. It was as though she was powerless to look away, mesmerised by the way he was allowing her to see so much of him. Not only was there a physical need but a mental and emotional one as well. It was as though he needed to connect with someone and he'd chosen to connect with her.

'Jennifer.' His other hand came up to caress her cheek and she leaned in to it, sighing at the gentle caress.

'What is this thing?' she whispered as her eyelids fluttering closed.

'I don't know but it's too good to ignore.'

She looked at him once more. 'But we should ignore it.'

'Why?'

'Because we work together.'

He shook his head. 'I'd like to say that's a lousy reason but . . .'

'But we both know we can't risk our working relationship by following this one.' Jennifer saw the logic breaking through his desire.

Jasper breathed in deeply. 'True.'

'And then there's the most important reason of all.'

Jasper raised an eyebrow in question.

'The girls,' she stated. 'If we start something and it doesn't work then the girls will get hurt, and they've already been through too much in their little lives.'

The fact that she cared so much about his daughters and their well-being spoke volumes about her. She was special, this fragile woman before him, and he wished that somehow they could figure out the puzzle before them.

'So where does that leave us?' He couldn't help but caress her cheek once more, knowing what she'd said was correct and totally logical, but he didn't want to be logical right at this moment. He wanted to start something . . . a *real* something which would lead to . . . Well, he wasn't exactly sure where. He certainly hadn't planned this intense attraction they felt for each other, and perhaps Jennifer was right, for now.

'Still at friends?'

For a moment, he stared at her as though she couldn't possibly be serious but he knew she was. He wanted more, though . . . or at least his heart did. His head, however, was prepared to do anything to protect his heart. He'd lived through so much pain, so much grief and while he'd picked up the pieces of his life and soldiered on, taking a step of this magnitude needed a clear head.

'I don't know, Jen. Sure . . . Of course we can be friends but I like seeing you. I like spending time with you. I really enjoyed our dinner the other night. No hospital. No children. No matchmaking friends. Just the two of us, and for the record, it's been a long time since I've felt totally comfortable with someone else while sharing a good meal.'

She nodded. 'I felt it, too, but, Jasper, what else can we do?' Jennifer held out her hands, palms up, indicating she was open to other suggestions. Jasper caught her hands in his and held them firmly.

'We're already colleagues and I hope we're becoming friends.'

'Yes,' she confirmed.

He didn't let go of her hands. Instead, he rubbed his thumbs over the backs of her knuckles, caressing them. Jennifer looked down, marvelling at the fact that she couldn't remember anyone ever touching her in such a caring yet intimate way. 'Right. Friends.' Jasper breathed in deeply, filling his lungs with the scent of her before somehow finding superhuman strength to break the contact. He stood, taking two steps away and raked a frustrated hand through his hair. 'For the record though, let it be noted that I'm *very* interested to see where this might lead . . . *if* we decide to be more than friends, I mean.'

Jennifer's body heated all the way through at his words and her eyes widened for a moment, wanting exactly the same thing, before she pulled herself together. She hadn't necessarily come back to Parramatta to start a romantic relationship. She'd come here to find herself, to reconcile her past and her present in the hope that she'd have a happier future. Building friendships *had* been part of her plan, and friendship was what she needed most from Jasper. Still . . . when he looked at her like that . . . When he said things like that . . . She swallowed over the dryness in her throat and nodded. 'Noted.'

'Anyway, none of this is helping you to make a decision about the house. You say that you're interested?'

'Most definitely. I'll get in contact with my solicitor and have the house inspected within the next few days. If everything checks out all right, I can't see why it wouldn't be perfect. It's close to the hospital, has somewhere for me to park the car, not too far from Sara's place . . .'

'Close to here. Er . . . I mean,' he began when he saw a puzzled look cross her face, 'it's good to have neighbours that you can turn to, can trust — in case of an emergency.'

'Of course.'

'And on your days off, you could always drop in and chat with my mother. She'd like that. Give her a short break from the girls.'

'Good. Well, yes. You're right. Those are definite pros.'

'Plus, we could car-pool some days. Save on petrol as well as greenhouse emissions.'

Jennifer grinned. 'You're just saying that in the hope of getting another drive of Miss Chief.'

Jasper matched her smile. 'Saw right through that ploy, didn't you?'

'Wasn't difficult.'

He met her look and held it. 'I'm so glad I could help out.' His tone was sincere and warmth spread through her. 'Really, I am. You're right, Jen. What we need is to be friends and not be overtaken by the frightening natural attraction we seem to feel for each other.'

'No . . . especially not when you put it that way.' Her words had become an intimate whisper and she quickly cleared her throat.

'I mean, I have the girls to consider. You have other demands on your time.' He was looking at her lips again, watching how they parted, how the air escaped from between them. How would they taste? He desperately wanted to know but as though he realised where his thoughts were heading yet again, he cut them off. Jennifer needed friends. He could tell there was still much of her past she hadn't dealt with and only time and good friendly support could get her through it. 'I'm glad I could help out with the house. That's one less thing you have to worry about.'

As he spoke, it was then Jennifer realised that he understood. He understood about Arturo and the connection she still felt with him. The past wasn't easy to put to rest and knowing he'd walked the path she was finally willing to face, to finally let go of the past, not only gave her confidence to take the next step but also increased her opinion of him. 'I'm glad you mentioned it to me. It really does seem as though it was meant to be. It has everything I need.'

'And it has a window-seat.'

She smiled then sighed. 'It does.' Jennifer paused for a moment. 'I like them, Jasper. They relax me. Strange how an inanimate object like a window-seat can relax someone in mind, body and spirit.'

Her eyes had taken on that far-off look again and Jasper didn't say anything, waiting to see if she was willing to share her thoughts with him. He didn't have to wait as long this time and he hoped it was because she was coming to trust him, to realise that he truly did understand what she was going through.

'I bought a house years ago with bay windows,' she said after a few minutes.

'Where?'

'Cherrybrook.'

'That's only a few suburbs over from here.'

'I know.'

'What happened?'

'I sold the house before I could move in.' Again Jasper remained quiet, waiting, giving her time to collect her thoughts. 'When I say that *I* bought the house, well, that's not strictly true. Arturo and I bought the house — together. We'd planned to move in after our honeymoon. We'd arranged to spend a good two weeks of our time off to set the house to rights, make it our own, set up my window-seat haven.'

As she spoke, she looked past him, as though she wasn't really seeing him any more but was lost in her memories. He knew all too well how that felt. 'What happened?'

'The cancer was more aggressive than we'd realised. When he was diagnosed, he had immediate surgery to remove the tumour. Then he had an aggressive course of chemotherapy and after all of that he finally started to improve. The wedding plans went ahead. When he was diagnosed with secondaries, he refused to cancel the wedding. He wanted to get married. He wanted me to be his wife.' She closed her eyes and shook her head. '*I* wanted to be his wife, more than anything. I loved him so much.'

Jasper desperately wanted to reach out and touch her but knew that if he did she might shatter into a million pieces. When you were sad like this, remembering and sharing your memories with someone new, sometimes the most simple act of kindness — a gentle touch on the hand, a reassuring hug — was enough to break the hard-to-maintain control Jennifer was now exhibiting.

'He died. Two days before the wedding. We had people coming in to town from overseas as well as interstate but, instead of attending a wedding, they ended up going to a funeral.'

No wonder she was so emotionally scarred. 'Jennifer.' He came to sit beside her again, his tone filled with empathy. He knew what she felt. He knew the pain. He knew the hurt.

She finally raised her eyes to his, one single solitary tear sliding down her cheek. He wanted to brush it away, to gather her close, to let her know he completely understood her desolation, but he didn't. 'Which makes Miss Chief all the more important,' he murmured. 'It maintains your link with Arturo and that's a good thing, Jen.' Jasper also realised his own good fortune in that moment because his link to Elisha, his daily reminder of his previous life, was in the form of two beautiful girls whom he adored.

She nodded at his words, pleased he hadn't tried to touch her. Part of her had wanted him to, had wanted him to hold her close, but she knew she would have broken down in tears and that was the last thing she needed. He would have offered comfort and right now she was too vulnerable not to take it. Instead, she had to remain focused on taking steps to move forward with her life, instead of living in the past and what might have been. Opening up to Jasper was one of those steps. He understood her so easily.

'How long had you been together?'

'We'd been together since our first week of medical school.' A small smile touched her lips. 'We met on the Monday and he asked me out on the Friday. He was persistent, especially as I was determined not to get involved with anyone due to the six long years of study that lay ahead of me. Art wouldn't take no for an answer. Halfway through first term he dropped out of medical school and studied education instead. Much more suited to his personality.' Her smile was bright, her eyes were shining with happiness, and Jasper's breath caught in his throat at the sight. She'd been a woman in love and all she had left were her memories. 'Art had a complete love of life. It was infectious and wherever we went everyone around him would end up having a fantastic time whether they wanted to or not.' She laughed softly. 'He pulled me out of my comfort zone, wanting me to try new things like abseiling and surfing and swimming with sharks.'

'Sharks?'

Jennifer nodded. 'Sharks. I was terrified but when it was over I felt so alive. And that was before you could go to some theme park and pay to swim with sharks in a tank. I'm talking about the ocean. Art never once begrudged the hard work it took to get me through medical school. He'd quiz me on anatomy, help me study before exams, even though he didn't have a clue what he was quizzing me on half the time.'

Jennifer looked up at Jasper and the light started to dim a little from her face. 'He was amazing. Just a normal high-school science teacher, not saving the world but making a huge difference in the lives of those he met. He introduced Matt and Sara.'

'Really?'

'Knew they were perfect for each other so

he got them together. That was my Arturo.'

'He sounds like quite a man.' There wasn't a hint of jealousy in his tone and she appreciated that. Arturo had been a part of her life, just as Elisha had been a part of his. She was pleased he knew there was no need to be jealous of a ghost.

'He was.' The light slowly vanished and sadness seemed to engulf her. 'And then he left me. My world crumbled and fell apart because he left me.'

'And you threw yourself into work.'

'I did. I had to find some way to gain control over my life again.' She raised her eyes to meet his. 'Work has been good to me. It gets me through. Helps me sleep.'

'Even now? All these years later?'

'Yes. Work is consuming.'

'But is it fulfilling?'

Jennifer thought about that but wasn't sure quite how to answer. Instead, she looked away and in an attempt to lighten the atmosphere, forced a small smile. 'Thank you for listening. It's very rare I talk about him.'

'Even with Sara?'

'Sara knew Art so I don't need to tell her how special he was. She already knows.'

'Talking about our loved ones, reliving memories, it helps bring them to life again . . . even for a few moments.'

'Exactly.' Jennifer nodded enthusiastically. 'I love it that you understand these feelings. That you're not jealous or overreacting to the power of a ghost.'

Jasper eyed her carefully for a second before venturing, 'They're not your words, Jen. Someone else has said that to you. A shrink, perhaps?'

'Am I that transparent?' She closed her eyes for a moment. 'I sort of started to get close to a colleague back in Melbourne who was a psychiatrist. That was about four years ago and he couldn't seem to understand that I needed my memories.'

'Many people don't. Sometimes all the textbooks in the world don't make a scrap of difference if they haven't experienced it.'

'I'm a different person now from whom I was back then, but it doesn't mean my past counts for nothing.'

'On the contrary, your past has helped make you into the person you are today.'

'Yes.'

'The fact that you've loved so deeply and then lost equally as deeply is something other people don't seem able to comprehend.'

'I take it you've tried to speak to other women about Elisha?'

Jasper nodded. 'They're naturally curious, I guess. Especially since I have children.'

Jennifer allowed herself a small smile. 'Most women are very nosy.'

He agreed. 'True, but whenever I'd start to answer their questions, to tell them about the girls or Elisha, they would feel as though it was some sort of competition, like they had to live up to the standards set by Elisha if they wanted to . . . to . . .' He searched for the right word. 'Secure me.'

'But that's not the case at all.'

'No. I would simply be answering their questions by telling them how incredibly wonderful the woman I married was.'

'Otherwise you wouldn't have married her.'

'Exactly.'

'So what was she like?' Jennifer had been curious about Elisha, as no doubt Jasper had been about Art.

'Blonde. Blue eyes.'

Jennifer's smile increased. 'I sort of gathered that by looking at the girls.'

'She was an interior designer who loved her job, loved creating atmospheres for people to live in. I think the best way to describe her was that she was content with who she was. I envied that to a certain degree. She was happy being a home body as well, supporting me through my studies, making sure I ate properly. I'd come home from work and invariably find the furniture rearranged or to find her painting the walls.'

'Did she decorate this place?'

'Yes, but over the years little changes have been made.'

'The girls following in their mother's footsteps?'

Jasper laughed. 'I guess you could say that especially as Lola did some . . . shall we say interesting artwork on her walls about three weeks ago.'

'Oh, no.'

'Oh, yes.'

'What did you do?'

'I hammered up a quick frame and hung it around the drawing. She was impressed.'

'I'm surprised she didn't do it again with that sort of reaction.'

'Lilly wanted to but I managed to convey my dislike of unauthorised murals and supplied them with a huge pile of paper instead.'

'They both like drawing?'

'Yes. Again taking after Elisha. I don't want them to lose that because they didn't know their mother.'

'She sounds delightful. I wish I could have met her.'

'Likewise with Arturo.'

'Thank you. I didn't mean to get so melancholy on you earlier.'

'Just having a bad day, eh?' Jasper nodded. 'I have them every now and then. Sometimes they creep up on you, other times it's around special occasions, anniversaries, that sort of thing, but at least then I'm more prepared.'

'So you have bad days, too?' Jennifer was a little surprised at that. 'I thought that was just me.' For some reason this news made her feel better instantly. It was as though she wasn't the only one who had bad days, days where she couldn't stop thinking about Art, about what their life would have been like together.

'I take it you didn't attend grief counselling afterwards?'

'I couldn't. I'm not the sort of person who can lay myself open to complete strangers. Sara wanted me to go but . . .' She shook her head. 'I couldn't. What I had with Art was private. Was about the two of us.'

'I'll bet you told yourself you were professionally trained to deal with grief, that you would figure it out sooner or later and that you didn't need a bunch of head-shrinkers telling you what you already knew.' As Jasper spoke, his words became softer, more personal, intimate. Jennifer watched him closely, noting the way his eyes had taken on a far-away look for a moment, as though he wasn't quite there.

'I take it you didn't go to counselling either?'

'No. Couldn't. It was too . . . personal.' He smiled and shook his head. 'Perhaps we're both over-achievers who think we know better?'

'I know I am — well, an over-achiever at any rate.' Her smile wasn't forced now, it was natural, and Jasper was completely taken with the way it lit up her face. His eyes skimmed her face, taking in the high cheekbones, the small smattering of freckles across the nose and the long eyelashes. Her hair was pulled back into the usual bun and the itching inside him, that yearning he'd been fighting for some time, the need to pull the pins free, to let the locks fall from their constraints and frame her face in the glorious way he instinctively knew they would, was becoming more difficult to re-sist.

What had begun as a friendly offer of compassion from someone who'd experi-enced similar emotions had now rapidly turned into a deeper awareness of each other. Jennifer could see a slight scar on

Jasper's chin which she'd never noticed before. It was barely hidden beneath his unshaven face but she saw it. The urge to reach out and trace her finger over the scar, to touch it, to ask about it, was unnerving as well as ridiculous.

They'd already agreed to just be friends, to be there and support each other. She had the feeling she could learn a lot from Jasper but for her own sanity, for her own peace of mind, she needed to keep things on a platonic level.

'I'd better get going.'

Her words broke the moment and Jasper moved away from her, knowing she was right.

'Breakfast and a look at the house. That was the . . . deal.' He'd almost said 'date'.

'It was, and can I just say again that those pancakes were totally amazing?' And so were you, she added silently.

'Thanks.'

'Well . . . I guess I'll go find the girls and say goodbye.'

'I think they're upstairs. If they're not, it means they've been too quiet for far too long and have no doubt done something they know I won't approve of.'

Jennifer smiled. 'Pure mischief, eh?'

'Yes. You have one Miss Chief but I have

two.' Jasper grinned as he led the way up the stairs to his parents' domain and there they found both girls drawing at the table, Iris sitting nearby, reading a book. Jennifer declined another cup of tea and said her goodbyes then Jasper walked her out to her car.

'Thanks again. For everything. Breakfast. The house. Listening.'

'It was my pleasure.' He leaned forward and pressed a friendly kiss to her cheek, but as he slowly pulled back and looked down into her face he realised it had been the wrong thing to do.

CHAPTER SIX

Two weeks later at the Friday morning clinic Jennifer was starting to get exhausted from all the extra running around. Several of the department's staff were off work, sick with colds and various forms of flu. It was a strong strain of bug which had hit the hospital hard this year and her department wasn't the only one suffering. Meetings had been cancelled, clinics were bursting at the seams and yet the hospital seemed to be operating with almost a skeleton staff.

After seeing thirty patients, she quickly spoke to the clinic sister before heading off to the cafeteria.

'Where are you going?' a deep voice said from behind her. Jennifer spun around, feeling almost guilty at leaving the clinic but it would only be for a few minutes.

'Jasper! You startled me.' He fell into step beside her.

'Coffee?' he asked, his steps as eager as

her own.

'Most definitely. It's just so busy that I need a little pick-me-up. My energy reserves are low and we still have half a clinic to get through. How about you?'

'Same. Although I did promise Louise I'd bring her back a coffee as well.'

She smiled. 'I promised Allan. In fact, I almost had to pull rank on him, he was so eager to get out for a few minutes.'

'The perks of being head of unit.'

'You could say that.'

'Yet how does it look that you're sneaking out to get coffee for yourself and the staff?'

'It looks as though I'm looking after them.' As they continued along the long corridor, she asked thoughtfully, 'Do you think I should requisition a coffee-machine to be installed in the clinic?'

'I think you'd win over the entire department as well as other departments that use that clinic area, not to mention the nursing and clerical staff.'

'We had one in the clinic in Melbourne.' They'd entered the cafeteria and headed for the coffee-machine.

'Was that your doing?'

'No. Someone else had done that before I arrived at the hospital but there were times too numerous to count that I silently thanked them for their forethought.'

'Well, if it helps, I'd gladly back up your decision.' Jasper nodded with firm resolution. 'Go to it, Dr Thorngate. Change the department, one coffee-machine at a time.' He leaned a little closer and his fresh, earthy scent enveloped her — the same fresh, earthy scent she'd been thinking about for weeks now. Jennifer breathed it in and tried not to close her eyes in delight. Being this near to Jasper was a definite pick-me-up and she suddenly wondered if she needed the coffee at all.

'Although . . .' His voice was rich and deep and wonderful. 'I feel compelled to warn you, if you *do* happen to requisition it and if it *does* happen, you may be in danger of losing your ice-queen status.'

Jennifer edged back a little, uncomfortable at being so near to him when it only made it more difficult for her to control the tantilising attraction that flowed through her. Pretending to consider his words, she paused thoughtfully before saying, 'Hmm. That would be worth considering. What if I put in a coffee-machine but increase everyone's workload? Do you think that might balance it out? I can be a saviour *and* still remain the ice queen.'

Jasper nodded thoughtfully. 'That might

work.' They paid for the drinks and headed back to clinic, sipping their own coffees along the way.

'As an alternative, I could fill in all the paperwork and get you to sign in the relevant places as though *you* were the instigator.'

'You'd let me take the glory for your brilliant idea?'

'If it meant ensuring most of the department were still afraid to approach me for any other funding requirements, sure.'

'Ah . . . well in that case, I think I have to tell you it may be a matter of too little, too late.'

'How so?'

'The registrars have already seen through your façade. They like you.'

'Oh, no.' Her expression was serious as she shook her head. 'That wasn't part of the plan.'

Jasper chuckled, liking the way she could keep a straight face. He made a mental note never to play poker against her. 'In fact, you've already won over both Allan and Louise. I think it might have been when you turned up for work the other day with flour on your nose and your hair a little out of place.'

'I was baking with your mother and the

girls. Lilly gave me one extra hug before I left to come in for the afternoon clinic and her fingers got caught in my hair. I didn't have time to tidy myself up. That's all.'

Jasper chuckled again. 'I was only teasing, Jen. Besides, it's good that people are seeing the real you.'

'It is?'

'Definitely.' He glanced over at her, his words warm. 'I like the real Jen Thorngate a lot better than the ice queen.'

'Hmm. I may have to rectify that situation. Remind me to leave an extra load of case notes on your desk before I leave.'

'It won't work. Everyone is saying that you're just what this department needs, that you're gifted when it comes to administration and that you're an excellent surgeon. I have to say, I agree with them. I'm sure if Maryanne wasn't so sick with this lurgy that she'd join the Jennifer Thorngate fan club.'

'Are you a card-carrying member?'

Jasper stopped just outside the clinic doors and gave her an intense look. His eyes had darkened to a smoky grey colour and Jennifer couldn't ignore the way her body sizzled with tingles. She parted her lips to let out her pent-up breath, her own eyes widening a little at his nearness.

'Jen. I'm the president.' His words were

soft but filled with meaning. His eyes dipped to her lips for a split second, causing another wave of tingles to flood her body before he walked through the clinic waiting room. She stood in the corridor, watching him through the glass until he disappeared from view down another side hallway.

He was the president of her fan club? What did that mean? She knew he was highly attracted to her, just as she was to him. They'd covered all of that a few weeks ago and until this moment he'd never even alluded to it since. What they hadn't covered was the fact that he'd kissed her. It had been a kiss on the cheek and a fleeting one at that but it had been enough to send her mind into a complete meltdown and leave her body whirling with need.

That kiss had been meant as a friendly gesture, a way of thanking her for opening up to him, but at the same time it had been Jasper's lips, brushing against her skin. His breath fanning softly over her and down her neck. It had been enough to take her dreams of him to another level, the one where he was kissing her, more thoroughly and far more often.

Jennifer closed her eyes, forcing her senses to return before following Jasper back into clinic, trying desperately to push his words and deep, penetrating looks aside, but it was becoming increasingly difficult. Still, she managed to achieve it to some degree and concentrated on her work rather than on the gorgeous, sexy man who was only three consulting rooms down from her own. She delivered coffee to a very grateful Allan before finishing off her own and calling her next patient through.

'Christopher.' She welcomed her nineteen-year-old patient back into the consulting room, accepting the X-ray packet from him. 'Now, let's see what's been happening with your hand.' She took the X-ray out and flicked on her viewing box. 'Ah . . . still not fully healed.' She pointed to where he had fractured his third and fourth metacarpals while he'd been skateboarding down a dimly lit road at three o'clock in the morning. 'When you come off your skateboard, you do a good job.'

'I really do.' Christopher was very interested in what she had to show him.

'I think you need to have the cast on for at least another fortnight. We'll do another check X-ray then to see if the healing has improved.'

'OK. So . . . I just make another appointment at the desk?'

'Yes. Get them to mark down that you're

to see me, specifically, for follow-up.'

' 'K.' Christopher returned to his chair and Jennifer went around the desk to write up the notes.

'Any other pain?'

'Nope.'

'Good.' She smiled at the young man she'd seen on her first day there. She stopped writing and fiddled with her pen. 'Can I just ask you, what were you doing skateboarding at three o'clock in the morning?'

'The question is, Doc, why weren't *you* skateboarding at three o'clock in the morning?'

Jennifer laughed and when the knock on her door came she immediately called for whoever it was to come in. A second later Jasper's broad shoulders filled the doorway. He looked from her, to her patient and then back again.

'Am I interrupting?'

'No. It's fine. Christopher was just about to tell me the *real* reason he was skateboarding at three o'clock in the morning.'

Jasper raised his eyes at that and looked with interest at the young man — the young man who'd made Jennifer laugh.

'It's the safest time,' Christopher said with a nonchalant shrug. 'You can see any cars that are coming sooner because you can see the headlights. The only reason I came off was I was going faster than I thought so when I jumped off the board my feet couldn't keep up.' He shrugged again and grinned from ear to ear, a love of life gleaming brightly in his eyes.

'Perhaps you shouldn't go so fast next time,' Jasper offered.

'It was the cape.'

'Cape?' both doctors asked in unison.

'Yeah. If you skateboard with a cape on, you go faster. You know, increase the wind velocity and all that. Superheroes rely on their capes to help them fly, to speed themselves up or slow themselves down. A cape is a must-have when skateboarding in the early morning hours.' His words were spoken with confidence and Jennifer admired him.

She glanced up at Jasper. 'It's a different world out there to when I was a teenager.' She shook her head, then looked again at Christopher, a smile on her face. 'Well . . . thank you for telling us.' She handed him a form. 'See you in two weeks and good luck with your uni exam next week. Thank goodness you didn't hurt the hand you write with.'

'Yeah. Then Mum would have been really

mad.' Christopher headed out, leaving Jasper standing there watching Jennifer.

'Cute kid,' she said as she signed her name to his notes and closed the file. 'Now, Jasper, what can I do for you?'

He held out an X-ray packet. 'Just wanted a second opinion on these.'

Jennifer stood and took the packet from him, pulling down Christopher's X-rays and putting them away before hooking up the ones Jasper had brought in. 'Lovely dislocation of the shoulder.'

'Does that look like a hairline fracture?' He pointed to the neck of humerus and Jennifer peered closer, squinting a little.

'Do you have another view?'

'Yes but it doesn't show up as clearly as this. I don't want to relocate the shoulder if it requires further stabilisation.' He paused, then said, 'You know that young boy probably has a crush on you.'

'Hmm? Oh, Christopher?' She looked up at Jasper and laughed. 'I doubt it. I'm far too old for him.'

'Nevertheless, he was looking at you as though he wanted to be your own personal superhero.'

Jennifer's face lit up with humour and the effect of her eyes and her hundred-watt smile were enough to make Jasper feel as though he'd been hit in the solar plexus.

'He reminded me of Arturo.'

'He looked like Arturo?'

'No.' She shook her head quickly. 'His love of life. Skateboarding at three o'clock in the morning is something Art would definitely have done — cape and all.'

'Crazy.'

'Oh, undoubtedly, and totally stupid as well but, still, that boy has a love of life, and when you think about it, it's not something we get to see all that often.'

'No. We get to see the after-effects.'

'Ooh. Grumpy Eddie, today, eh? Perhaps you need another coffee?'

'I am *not* grumpy,' he protested. He was secretly pleased Jennifer was teasing him in such a manner and also that she was opening up about Arturo. After their deep and meaningful discussion he'd wondered if she'd treat him any differently at work. At first it had appeared the ice-queen was in residence as they'd done ward round together but later on when they'd been in clinic she'd smiled at him. Why he'd felt as though the sun had come out from behind a cloud he wasn't sure, but that was the way he'd felt for the past two weeks. When she smiled at him, as she was doing now, he couldn't help but enjoy it. Unfortunately, they'd been too busy to spend any quality time together, something he'd planned on doing. After all, he'd told himself several times, friends were allowed to spend time together. Weren't they? Still, he had two tickets to a concert that evening, burning a hole in his pocket. He hadn't said anything to her about it, unsure of emergencies, but if it turned out they were both free tonight, he was definitely going to try and persuade her to accompany him. He'd already primed the girls and his mother not to expect him back for dinner. He glanced at her . . . hoping things turned out his way.

'No. Just sounding old,' she countered.

'Thank you very much.'

Jennifer laughed again and placed a hand on his arm. 'I didn't mean it like that. You're only two years older than I am so it wouldn't do me much good to rib you about your age.'

'No, it wouldn't.' He looked down at where her hand rested on his arm, feeling the warmth, her humour and her natural ability to care. Jennifer was the type of person who didn't want anything to be misconstrued if she could help it. Jasper had also realised that not many people got to see this side of her yet she was allowing him to. It made him feel quite privileged.

As though she realised she was touching him, she quickly removed her hand, hoping he didn't think she was making a pass at him or leading him on in some way. Slowly, she raised her eyes to meet his and found him smiling. Letting out the small breath she'd been holding, she watched as he crossed his muscled arms over his chest, the fabric of his cotton shirt pulling taut over his biceps.

'Who told you my age?'

Jennifer, trying desperately to ignore the way her body responded to his, opened her mouth to answer, but he'd already figured it out.

'Sara,' he continued.

'Well, yes, but it's also in your personnel file.' Her eyes widened as she realised he might take that the wrong way.

'Been checking on my academic transcript, boss?'

Jennifer lifted her chin slightly and Jasper couldn't help but smile. He was coming to love it when she did that.

'I've been checking up on *all* my staff, if you must know.' But she wouldn't tell him she'd pored over every aspect of his for quite some time. It was as though she was becoming obsessed with him, with wanting to know everything about him, thinking about him . . . dreaming about him. 'It's not uncommon for a new head of unit to want to know the capabilities of the staff, both practically and academically.'

'No. Not uncommon at all.' He was still smiling and he sounded as though he didn't believe her one little bit but, thankfully, it appeared he was going to let her get away with it. They stood there, looking at each other, the atmosphere intensifying. She needed to break the moment. She knew that but the signals her brain was sending to her limbs, particularly her legs, that they should move were being interrupted by the hypnotic way Jasper was looking at her.

'Uh . . . Jen.' He cleared his throat, surprised to find he was a little nervous about asking her out.

'Mmm?'

'Are you free this evening?'

Her eyebrows raised. 'Free?'

'Not busy? And I'm not talking about paperwork. That is not a valid excuse.'

'What would be a valid excuse, then?'

'An emergency.'

She waited for him to give her other options but none were forthcoming. 'That's it? An emergency is my only form of excuse?'

'Yes.' He smiled, feeling more sure of himself. 'Anyway, I have tickets.' He dug into his trouser pocket and pulled out two tickets, showing her. 'It's for a concert tonight at the Sydney Opera House and I just thought that if you weren't . . .'

Jennifer took a ticket from him and examined it more closely. 'Rock 'n' roll classics?'

'It's not opera or anything like that. It's just different well-known Australian bands playing their favourite rock 'n' roll classics. Given that you like that period of music so well, I just thought . . .' he shrugged '. . . that you might like to go.'

Jennifer looked at the ticket and then back at Jasper. 'You bought tickets?'

'Obviously.'

'When?'

'Two days ago. I wasn't sure what the rosters would be, given people were off sick.'

'Fair enough.'

'So?' he prompted, when she didn't say anything else, still staring at the ticket as though she couldn't quite believe it. 'Would you like to go?'

Jennifer nodded, excited by not only the prospect of going to a concert — something she hadn't done since she'd been a med student — but of going with Jasper. 'Yes, please.'

Jasper couldn't believe the relief he felt at her answer. 'Great. Excellent.' He indicated the ticket in her hand. 'Do you want to hold onto that or would you like me to keep it for you?'

'Keep them together.' She handed it back. 'They're a pair.'

He grinned at her words. 'Yes, they are.' Was that an indication that she was ready to take their own relationship up another step? To be a pair? He certainly hoped so. 'I'll start praying for no big emergencies tonight.'

'You do that because there are some fantastic bands in that line-up.'

Jasper shook his head. 'You really are quite a surprising woman, Dr Thorngate.'

'Thanks. I think.' She looked up at him, the distance between them still the same as before but she knew in accepting this invitation from him she'd just raised the bar on their friendship . . . and she was actually quite happy about it. 'Do you want to meet for dinner before the show?'

'I was just about to ask that. Sure. That would be great.'

'OK. First, though, I'd suggest we get through the rest of this day, and the first step will be getting your patient X-rayed again.' She turned and walked back to her desk, needing to put some distance between them because whenever she found herself close to Jasper like that it was becoming far more difficult not to reach out and slip her arms about his waist. She had a date with him tonight. A real live date and she couldn't wait.

'That was my thought but, again, as head of unit I didn't know whether that would be considered as not adhering to cost-effective means.'

His words helped bring her mind back onto the right track. 'If the patient requires further X-ray then they should be entitled to it. Better to spend the money doing that rather than risk a lawsuit for ineffective treatment — or, worse, the wrong treatment.'

He looked at her for a moment, pleased with what he was hearing. 'Agreed.'

'Then why do you seem so surprised at my recommendation? Was my predecessor a penny-pincher?'

'You could say that.'

'Ah, well, no wonder I have a fan club.' And he was president. She tried not to smile at the thought. 'Wait a minute. Why is someone presenting to clinic with a dislocated shoulder?'

'They didn't. It was an A and E call requiring an orthopaedic consult.'

'But you're not on call. Louise is.'

'Louise isn't feeling too well and was only just managing to cope with clinic. When the call came in, I took it.'

'No wonder you needed coffee. Keep me informed on Louise's health, if you wouldn't mind.'

Jasper shook his head and tut-tutted. 'You're never going to keep up your ice-queen persona if you keep caring about your staff in this way.'

'I'm a doctor. It's my job to care.'

'Yes, but you're also the department administrator. It's your job to squeeze the most out of your staff and protect all unnecessary expenditure.'

'And after one whole month of being here, I'm well under budget — but don't let that get around.'

Jasper pretended to zip his lips. 'My lips are sealed,' he mumbled, making her laugh. He was delighted at the sound.

'Besides, if you act as my go-between guy, then I can keep my ice-queen image as well as surreptitiously caring for my staff.'

'You want me to spy for you?'

'Only on the important things.'

'Such as . . .'

'The need for a coffee-machine in the clinic, but more prominent would be the health of our colleagues.' When he raised an eyebrow, she pressed on. 'They hardly know me, Jasper and I'm just not good with the nitty-gritty personal stuff. Yes, I care if people are sick and suggest they actually take the sick leave they've no doubt accrued to get better. The department will manage as best as it can. No one is indispensable and I truly believe that's the biggest flaw most of us doctors have. We always think we're totally irreplaceable and therefore refuse to take a day off to actually get better. Instead, we come to work, spread our germs around to all and sundry and then wonder why we're not getting any better. Yet if we simply followed the advice we give to our patients — i.e. go home, rest and drink plenty of fluids — we'd be back at work in no time.'

'Whew! Don't hold back, Jen. Tell me what you really think.'

Jennifer smiled at his words. 'Sorry. The head of unit I worked under in Melbourne was a bully, in my opinion, for not allowing his staff days off despite the fact they were ready to drop from total exhaustion. That is *not* effective management, neither is it effective medicine, and it's *that* type of defective management that leads to lawsuits.'

'You have a real thing about avoiding lawsuits.'

'I do and personally I think it's a good trait for an administrator to have. If staff are healthy and alert —'

'Translate — take days off and drink coffee when working . . . Continue.'

'Then the department will run more smoothly. Patients will receive the care they need and everyone's happy.'

'Except for the lawyers. You're leaving them with nothing to do.'

Jennifer smiled up at him and once more Jasper took a hit to his solar plexus. The woman was starting to really consume his thoughts. In the mornings he'd wonder what she was going to wear to work. At lunch he'd listen to his colleagues sing her praises, all of them totally surprised at how brilliant she was. In the evening he would wonder what she looked like as she dressed for bed, with her dark locks flowing loosely around her shoulders, softening the gorgeous structure of her face. Then he'd dream of her. Dream of kissing her. No woman had consumed him so much since he'd first met Elisha.

Jasper belatedly realised he was staring and turned away, collecting the X-rays and putting them back into the packet. 'Um . . .' He paused at the door. 'Are you going tomorrow?'

'Tomorrow?'

'To Sara's mid-winter barbecue.'

'Oh, that. Yes. I'm going. Are you?' She'd been wondering if she'd see him there or, more to the point, she'd been hoping she'd see him there.

'Yes. The girls are very excited about it.'

'No doubt.'

'My parents will be there too, and Megan, if she can make it.'

'Great. I'm looking forward to meeting your sister. How are the wedding plans going?'

'Frantic, from what Mum says. I haven't had the courage to even broach the subject with my little sis. Besides, she has enough stress on her plate.'

'Did the girls' dresses show up?'

'Yes. They've had their final fitting and look like adorable little angels.'

'I'm sure they do. Do the dresses come complete with halos?'

Jasper chuckled. 'No, thank goodness, or those halos would definitely be slipping a bit on my two girls.'

'They're adorable, Jasper, and you know it.'

'Adorable? Yes. A handful? Yes. Able to walk slowly down the aisle? No.'

'They're four. What do you expect?'

'I expect Megan's beginning to regret asking them.'

'It will all be fine on the day.'

'You think so?' He exhaled and fiddled with his tie, smoothing it down. 'I hope so. I don't want to disappoint Megan.'

'Well, it's not your fault if you have two adorable but unruly children. Oh, wait a minute, it is,' she joked, and Jasper merely rolled his eyes and shook his head. 'How about if we have a practice tomorrow at Sara's place? I'm sure Sara and I can explain it to them, how they need to be perfect young ladies and walk like princesses.'

'Good luck.'

'It'll be fine,' she repeated. 'You're just struggling because you don't know how to speak female.'

'Thank goodness you're fluent in it.'

'Yes.' There was a knock on the consulting-room door and the clinic sister poked her head in.

'There the two of you are. There are patients everywhere and you're standing around gas-bagging. Get back to work.'

'Yes, Sister,' they both replied, dutifully chastised. As the sister headed off, Jasper and Jennifer smiled at each other, no words needed as they communicated they were glad they'd had these few minutes alone.

'Action stations,' Jasper said, and winked at her before he left. Jennifer stood where she was for a second, waiting for her heart rate to return to normal, unable to believe the way he affected her. When she felt the lub-dub of her heart was more sedate, she headed to the waiting room to call her next patient through and realised her energy was completely restored. Five minutes in Jasper's company had done more than all the coffee she'd drunk so far that morning and she was starting to believe *he* was the healthier option.

CHAPTER SEVEN

Dinner had been lovely. The concert had been amazing and as they walked to Jennifer's car, she was bouncing with life.

'That was . . . so incredibly brilliant.'

'It was,' Jasper agreed. He'd taken her hand as they'd headed out of the venue, not wanting to lose her in the throng of people making their way down the steps of the Sydney Opera House . . . and he hadn't let go. It also appeared that Jennifer was more than happy for him to continue holding her hand.

They were both dressed casually in jeans and jumpers, their coats now around them to protect from the cool evening wind. Jennifer hadn't worn her hair loose, as he'd hoped, but it wasn't in her usual bun either. Instead, she'd pulled it back into a French braid, keeping it tidy and out of the way.

'That guitarist — the one who came running through the audience and then jumped up on the small stage at the back and did his guitar solo . . .' She squeezed his hand tight and even wrapped her other hand about his arm, drawing him even closer. 'Wow. It was just . . . Wow.'

He laughed and decided it was the perfect opportunity to let go of her hand, but only to slip his arm around her shoulders. She didn't stop him, instead sliding her own arm around his waist.

'Thank you so much for bringing me, Jasper.'

'It was my pleasure.' He looked down and winked at her as they continued to the car park. 'Although I have to say I don't think I've ever seen you this animated before.'

'That's because I haven't felt this alive in years, and I mean years, Jasper. I knew coming back to Parramatta would help with the healing, but I hadn't expected to find this.' She hugged him close.

'This?'

'This bond we seem to be forging. It was the nicest thing in the world for you to get the tickets, to invite me when you knew I liked classic rock 'n' roll. It was so thoughtful. So caring.' She stopped walking in the middle of the footpath, pulling him to a halt before leaning up to press a kiss to his cheek. 'Thank you.'

Jasper put his other arm around her, pulling her closer, both of them uncaring of other people who were now having to walk around them. 'Jennifer.' He'd wanted this moment for so long, to be holding her close like this, to feel her breath mingling with his, and now that it was here he wanted to savour it, to memorise it. 'I'm not sure whether —'

'Shh.' She placed a finger over his lips before sliding her hand around his neck, her fingers lacing into his hair as she urged his head down. 'Kiss me, Jasper. Just kiss me.'

'Never argue when the woman's right,' he murmured in that moment before his lips touched hers for the very first time. The moment was electrifying, mind-numbing and, oh, so perfect. Her lips were the most perfect fit for his own. His mind was most definitely numb and the energy, the need pulsing between them could have been harnessed to power a small city.

She tasted like the night, dark, sleek and seductive, and the one thing that gave him hope that what he was feeling for her wasn't just that of a passing fancy, was that neither of them had consumed any alcohol that evening. With not knowing if they'd be called to an emergency, it had seemed the wise course of action but now he was pleased because it meant her reaction to him was real. There were no inhibitors making her act out of the ordinary. The woman he held in his arms, the woman whose mouth was pressed so firmly to his own in the most sweetest and seductive kiss he'd ever experienced, was happy to be with him.

When they broke apart, neither of them spoke. It was as though the emotions had been too powerful, too strong for them to process in that moment, and they continued to the car park. Jasper drove the Jaguar back towards Parramatta, holding Jennifer's hand firmly in his own.

When he turned into her driveway and cut the engine, he turned to face her. 'Jennifer.'

'Hmm?'

He could see she was tired and drowsy, coming down from her earlier euphoric high. It made him realise that now wasn't the time for a talk. They were both tired. Both had a busy day tomorrow and both needed sleep. Still . . . tonight had changed things and he needed her to acknowledge that.

'I had a really good time tonight.' He brought her hand to his lips and kissed it, relieved when she smiled.

'Me, too. It was . . . exactly what I needed.'

'Really?'

'Yes.' She gestured to her house with a jerk of her thumb. 'Want to come in for a cup of tea?'

'Are you awake enough to make it?' he quizzed.

'Probably not, so I should say that if you accept my invitation, *you'll* be making the tea.'

He chuckled and leaned forward to brush a kiss over her lips, thrilled when she didn't pull away or tense up. If anything, she seemed to relax more, sighing into him, her breathing even, her eyes closed. 'You're exhausted,' he declared.

'Mmm.'

'I'll pass on the tea.' He climbed from the car, coming around to the passenger side to open the door for her. When the cool night air hit her, though, she was instantly alert.

'I had the most wonderful time, Jasper. Thank you for asking me,' she said again.

'Thank you for accepting.' He pulled her into his arms and she snuggled into his warmth.

'Mmm. You smell nice.'

'So do you.'

'Are you sure you don't want a cup of tea?'

Jasper swallowed and looked at her dark house, then looked at her, illuminated by

170

the distant porch light which was casting a soft amber glow over them. 'I don't think that's a good idea just yet.'

'It's just tea, Jasper.'

'You and I both know that's not the case, Jen. Sure, we might drink tea but then things would escalate and end up leading us in a direction I don't think either of us is ready for just yet.'

She pulled back to look at him, raising her eyebrows. 'You're very sure of yourself.'

He grinned. 'I'm sure of where we both know this will eventually end . . . one day.'

'But not tonight,' she stated.

'No. Not tonight. However, things have changed, Jen. You know that, right?'

'I do. Things have changed, Jasper, and you have no idea how happy I am about that. What I also need, though, is time to process this change.'

'Agreed.' He brushed his lips across hers once more. 'I'll see you at Sara's barbecue tomorrow?'

'Yes. You and me with, no doubt, quite a few pairs of eyes watching us to see how we behave.'

'We'll have to be careful. Not that I'm suggesting we hide from this.'

'No. I understand. We need to be careful. There are other people involved in this and perhaps keeping things to ourselves is the best option for now.'

'For now.' With great reluctance Jasper let her go, holding her hand as he walked slowly backwards until he couldn't hold on any more. 'For now,' he reiterated, before disappearing into the night.

Jennifer rang the doorbell a second time, gripping the shopping bags tightly so she didn't drop them. 'Come on, come on,' she muttered. It would be too much effort to put the bags down, open the door and pick the bags up again but it appeared, as no one was coming to answer the door, that that was exactly what she had to do.

'Coming!' she heard, and in the next instant Sara's front door was thrown open and Jasper stood there, looking gorgeous in dark denim jeans, which had long since forgotten any shape but his, and a thick Aran jumper. He looked . . . delicious and for a split second Jennifer's mind went blank.

They both stood there, staring at each other, Jasper shaken because Jennifer's hair wasn't pulled back in its usual severe bun. It was still back but she'd pulled it loosely into a ponytail and the ends of her dark hair were currently hanging over one shoulder, a few strands coming loose here and there. Her cheeks were pink from the cool breeze and her eyes were bright and glorious. She was beautiful. It was only when she shifted a shopping bag that he snapped out of his trance and offered his help.

'Here. Let me take them from you.' He started forward, which was enough to bring her back to reality. She gripped the bags tighter.

'I've got them. If I let go, I might end up dropping them.'

He shifted back to make way for her and she quickly headed into the kitchen, dumping the bags on the bench. 'I was wondering where you were,' Jasper commented as Jennifer began unpacking the items.

'Sara had run out of a few things.' She held up a large bottle of tomato sauce to prove her point.

'A key item,' he agreed. 'How can you have a barbecue without tomato sauce, especially in Australia?'

'Hence why I went to the shops. Sara's boys go through the sauce like it's a drink.'

'It is an Aussie staple.'

'True.'

They worked alongside each other, Jasper taking the items from the bags and Jennifer putting them away or out where they needed to be.

'You look nice,' he remarked as she closed the fridge door.

'Oh?' Jennifer stopped and looked down. It was then she realised she was still wearing her scarf and coat. 'No wonder I was so warm.' She unwound her scarf and was pleasantly surprised when Jasper helped her off with her coat. It reminded her of her first morning at work when he'd helped her on with her white clinical coat. Why did it seem so long ago? He carefully put her garments over the back of a nearby chair and looked at her again.

'I like your hair.'

Consciously, Jennifer raised a hand to her hair and twirled her ponytail through her fingers.

He swallowed over the sudden dryness of his throat. Was he allowed to say things like that to her? He wasn't quite sure where they stood in that department but he simply hadn't been able to stop himself from commenting. 'It's . . . uh . . . longer than I thought.' As well as being more rich and glorious than he'd imagined. The pale pink cashmere jumper she wore only made the blue of her eyes more vivid. The indigo of her jeans and the black boots with the small heel topped off her outfit and Jasper's mouth became even drier as he allowed himself one more appraisal of her gorgeous body.

'Jasper.' Heat had flowed through her as his gaze had wandered over her.

'Jennifer.' When he lifted his eyes to meet hers, he wasn't surprised to discover repressed desire in her blue depths. He also knew she could see the same emotion in him.

'Don't look at me that way.'

'You've said that before but I just don't seem to be able to stop.' His voice had dipped to an intimate whisper and somehow the distance between them had seemed to disappear.

'We can't.'

'Why not?'

'Not here. Too many eyes.' She glanced around her as she spoke, checking to see there weren't any other guests . . . or Sara . . . lurking around the corner, listening to everything they said. 'And this is hardly the time to continue our discussion. Standing in the middle of Sara's kitchen.'

'True.' Jasper exhaled harshly and shoved his hands in his pockets, desperate to control the need to haul her into his arms. 'Tomorrow?'

'Sorry?'

'Can we discuss this tomorrow?'

'I'm on call.'

'I'll come to the hospital and help you if I have to, just so long as I can get ten minutes alone with you between cases.'

'Jasper.'

'Jen, I can't stop thinking about you. It's starting to drive me insane.'

'I . . . er . . . can't stop thinking about you either.' A slight blush tinged her cheeks at the words.

His eyebrows raised at this information and the corners of his lips tugged into a small smile. 'Really?'

'Yes. Why are you so surprised?'

'I'm not surprised. I'm . . . very pleased by this information. It means we're both on the same page.'

'Page? What page?' A woman with short blonde hair and large circles beneath her eyes came into the kitchen. 'Have you joined a book club, big brother?' She laughed at her own joke. 'As if you'd have time for reading anything that isn't a medical text. That's all I have time for. That and stupid bridal magazines.'

Jennifer had stepped back, putting distance between the two of them as the woman who was obviously Jasper's sister had come into the kitchen.

'Jennifer, this is my sister Megan. Megan, this is Jennifer, my new boss at the hospital.'

'Oh, hi. I've heard so much about you.' Megan shook hands with Jennifer.

'You have?' She looked to Jasper. Had he confided in his sister?

'The girls told Megan how you came over for pancakes,' he quickly clarified, seeing the look of panic that had crossed Jennifer's face.

'Pancakes.' Megan said the word and nodded knowingly, as though 'pancakes' was a code word for something completely different.

'They were delicious,' Jennifer said, trying to make the point that pancakes had definitely been on the menu rather than what Megan was insinuating . . . even though Megan wasn't at all far from the truth.

'That's how it starts,' Megan continued, not fooled for a second. 'Pancakes one minute, marriage proposal the next, and then, wham — a week before the wedding the groom isn't sure he wants to go through with it.'

'What?' Jasper put his hands on Megan's shoulders, instantly concerned. 'Megsy? What's happened?'

At that question Megan burst into tears

and buried her face in her brother's chest, his arms automatically going around her. He met Jennifer's eyes over the top of his sister's head and smiled sadly. 'Tomorrow,' he mouthed, and Jennifer nodded, leaving the kitchen to give them some privacy. She admired the way he was there to support his sister, to comfort her and to help her through what was obviously a difficult time. He was quite a man.

Jennifer busied herself helping Iris and talking to Ian, Jasper's father, as he cooked the meat, chicken and prawns on the barbecue. Most of the people there were related in some obscure way or, like Jennifer herself, were old friends of either Sara or Matt. There were children everywhere and lots of fun and laughter, and it was just the sort of day Jennifer needed after the past hectic month.

'Still working day and night?' Iris asked a while later, coming to sit with Jennifer beneath the small marquee in the back yard. The two of them had seen each other a few times during the past week after Jennifer had moved into her new home. The first time she'd popped in, Iris had brought a cake to officially welcome Jennifer to the neighbourhood, and along with the cake had come two adorable girls to help eat it.

Both Lola and Lilly had ended up with chocolate smeared all over their faces, hands and Jennifer's glass tabletop. It had been then she'd realised that her furniture was hardly child friendly and she'd made a mental note to child-proof the house so the twins would be safe when they visited.

'Working day and night and night and day but I feel as though I'm finally starting to get things under control. Sort of.' Jennifer smiled.

'You have a lovely smile, dear, and I do like the way you're wearing your hair. It suits you. Highlights your pretty eyes.'

'Oh. Thank you.' It was strange for Jennifer to receive compliments like that, especially since her own mother had never taken the time to give her any.

Iris leaned a little closer and spoke in an intimate whisper. 'I think Jasper likes your hair like that, too.'

Jennifer nodded slowly. 'He did mention it.'

'Did he?' Iris's eyebrows lifted at this news. 'The two of you becoming . . . better acquainted?'

For the second time since she'd arrived, Jennifer felt her cheeks tinge with colour and she lowered her head, a little embarrassed.

'Don't misunderstand me, Jennifer. I think it's wonderful. Jasper needs someone like you and the more I get to know of you, the more I'm thinking that you need someone like Jasper.'

'Hmm.' She fiddled with the ring she wore on her right hand, still unable to look at Iris, hoping the woman would change the subject.

'I saw you having a lovely tête-à-tête with Jasper earlier. I could have screamed at Megan for interrupting you. It looked as though you were about to kiss.'

'Iris, I'm —'

'I know, I know.' Iris patted Jennifer's hand. 'It's none of my business but I do want him to be happy. It's what every mother wants for their children. For them to be happy in love.' She sighed, her gaze coming to rest on Megan.

'How's she doing?' Jennifer was glad of the reprieve.

'Not as well as you and Jasper, I'm afraid. Poor Megan. Ian and I aren't particularly happy with her choice of marriage partner — Megsy's far too good for him — but she says she's in love and despite how much heartache the cad seems to cause her, she forgives him.'

'Love's a tricky thing.' Jennifer's words

were spoken softly and Iris gasped as she absorbed their true meaning.

'You've been in love before,' she stated. 'Well, no wonder you want to take things slowly with my son. Good for you and good for him.' Iris placed her hand on Jennifer's. 'Just know that if you want to talk about anything, anything at all, you can bend my ear any time, dear.'

Jennifer was so touched by the heartfelt words that tears sprang into her eyes. 'Thank you, Iris.'

'Oh, no, dear. Have I said something wrong? I didn't mean to upset you.'

'It's not that. It's just . . . my mother and I don't . . .' She stopped and sniffed. 'Well, let's just say we're not at all close. I guess that's why I'm not all that good at relationships.'

'Oh, toffle. You have a brilliant and long-lasting friendship with Sara, don't you? And Matt? What about their boys? And Lilly and Lola can't stop talking about you. Jasper says you're doing fantastic things for the department and I know for a fact that *he's* quite taken with you. If that's not having relationships, personal or otherwise, I don't know what is.'

'But I'm not good at communicating.'

Iris scoffed. 'What do you call this, then?'

She indicated the space between the two of them. 'You don't give yourself nearly enough credit, Jennifer.'

'That's what I keep telling her,' Jasper remarked as he entered the marquee. He'd been watching Jennifer and his mother talking for quite a few minutes now and was growing restless to know what they were talking about. Was his mother sticking her nose in where it didn't belong? Was she scaring Jennifer off? It was those thoughts which had made him walk over and pull up a chair on the other side of Jennifer, shifting it a little closer before he sat. As he breathed in, her fresh perfume surrounded him and he felt himself relax. The woman really did have an amazing effect on him.

'Do you know, she requisitioned a coffee-machine for the clinic and made me put it all in my name?' Jasper shook his head as though she was a lost cause. 'I just don't know what to do with you, Dr Thorngate.'

Iris stood and grinned. 'I can think of a few things.' She winked at them both.

'Mum!' Jasper was momentarily mortified but then laughed as he watched his mother head over to talk to Sara. Well, at least he now knew his mother was definitely on his side. 'Sorry about her.'

Jennifer smiled at him. 'It's all right. I

think it's nice that she can tease you.'

'She was teasing you, too.'

'Was she?' Jennifer couldn't contain her surprise. 'I don't think I've ever been teased by someone else's mother before.'

'Were you close to Arturo's parents?'

'It was just Art and his dad at the time but his father passed away about a year after Art's death.' She paused. 'What about Elisha's parents? Do you see them?'

'The girls have only seen them once. They live in Canada so it's a bit difficult for them to be a part of their lives, but they send birthday money and Christmas cards.'

'A shame, really.' Both looked over to where the girls were running around with Sara's boys, giggling brightly.

'It is.' They were silent for a few minutes, both completely comfortable without feeling pressed to make conversation. It was a nice feeling. 'Now, I've been meaning to ask, how is everything going in your new home?'

'It's . . . cosy.'

Jasper leaned his elbow on the armrest and came closer. 'And the window-seat?'

Her smile increased. 'Relaxing.'

He straightened. 'Excellent. So when is it your turn to have us around for breakfast?'

'I'm sorry?'

'Well, you've been to my place for pancakes. A good neighbour always returns the invitation. It says so in the etiquette book.'

That made Jennifer laugh and he loved the way it seemed to brighten the entire marquee. 'You've actually read an etiquette book?'

'Well . . . no, but my mother has and that's what she's told me all my life.'

'Oh, well, if it's in the etiquette book, I guess we'd better sort out a date. Now, by "us" do you mean you and the girls or should I include your parents in this invitation? After all, your mother has dropped by a few times to visit on my days off.'

He nodded slowly. 'She did mention that. As far as who to invite, personally I think you should have three different events. One with just me. Then one with myself and the girls and then one with the whole family.'

'Just you, eh? The two of us? Eating breakfast alone?' She raised an eyebrow. 'I don't honestly think the girls will let you, Jasper.'

'You're probably right.'

'And I didn't have breakfast alone with you last time — the girls were there as well.'

'I know, I know.' He shifted uneasily in his chair. 'I guess I'm just impatient to get some time alone with you. To talk.'

'We will. Tomorrow. You're going to snatch

ten minutes of my time between A and E cases, remember?'

'Or we could have breakfast bright and early tomorrow morning before you go to work.'

Jennifer bit her lip at the suggestion, so desperately wanting to give in, to accept, but knowing once she was alone with Jasper in such a secluded environment, anything could happen.

'Or I could just come to the hospital.' He went back to his earlier suggestion. 'I could power through some of your paperwork for you so that when Martha comes in on Monday morning, your reputation as a slave driver would remain intact.'

'The poor woman would probably have a heart attack and I seriously don't want that.'

'I can still help and we can talk in between funding applications,' he suggested, a teasing light in his eyes.

Jennifer chuckled. 'How utterly romantic. And then once the paperwork's done, I suppose we can talk between patients and mop-up lists.'

'We could. At least I'd get to be with you.'

She looked into his eyes as he spoke and couldn't stop her breath from catching in her throat at the repressed desire she saw there.

'The sooner we talk, Jen, the better.'

'For who?' she whispered.

'For both of us.' He reached out and took her hand. 'How about tonight?'

'So, Jennifer.' Megan barrelled in to the marquee and Jennifer instantly shifted, letting go of Jasper's hand. Jasper could have cheerfully throttled his sister.

Megan sat in the seat her mother had recently vacated. 'Jasper tells me you're the new head of unit and you're only the same age as me. You must have worked very hard.'

'I have.'

'Congrats on the dream job, then.'

'Thanks.'

'You could have been head of your unit long ago,' Jasper felt compelled to point out to his sister, trying to hide his annoyance at her bad timing. 'You're a bright spark. Where do you think the girls get it from?'

'Er . . . you. You're no dummy, Jasp. Anyway, like you, big brother, I'm not one for administrative work. It takes a special kind of doctor to juggle both admin and medicine.'

'Jennifer is that doctor,' Jasper said, proudly and Jennifer smiled at him, warmed by the look in his eyes. He wanted to talk to her, to *seriously* talk about the attraction between them. Even the thought of having that conversation was enough to set the butterflies churning in her stomach. Excited by the prospect, she wasn't quite sure what to do. Should she agree to see him tonight? Wouldn't it be dangerous for him to come over in the evening when the girls were asleep? Would they be able to control the desires that were building every moment they spent together?

It was a big step and she wasn't sure she had the courage to take it.

'Hello?' Megan waved her hand and snapped her fingers between the two of them, a happy smile on her face. Jennifer was amazed at how it changed her appearance, how it made the dark circles beneath her eyes disappear, made her blue eyes sparkle and her straight, white teeth show. She looked for similarities between the siblings but only found it in the nose and ears. 'Gee. You two are worse than me and Calvin. That's my fiancé,' she clarified for Jennifer's sake. 'He's also good at admin and medicine. He's head of Cardiothoracic at Sydney General.'

'Oh. OK.' Jennifer watched as Megan frowned a little as she spoke. The light went out of her eyes, her face took on a dark scowl and a moment later she excused herself. 'Is she all right?' Jennifer was genuinely concerned.

'I'm not sure.'

'You said she's doing most of the planning herself?'

'Most? Try all.'

'Why doesn't she hire a wedding consultant?'

'Megan? Megan only asks for help as a last resort. It's one of her biggest faults.'

'And her fiancé isn't helping at all?'

'No. He doesn't want anything to do with it. Just told her to tell him where and when he should turn up, but from what she said earlier he's even having second thoughts about doing that.'

'A lot of people get cold feet.'

'Would you have been one?'

'No.' She wasn't hurt by the question. They'd been open and honest with each other about their pasts. 'How about you?'

'Nope. Unfortunately, though, my darling sister is a bit of a control freak, in the nicest sense of the word. She's not domineering. She just likes things done her way, especially when it comes to things like her wedding.'

'Well, most girls start to plan their wedding at about age twelve.'

'Did you?'

'Of course.'

'Has it changed over the years?'

Jennifer thought for a moment. 'Here and there, but I think that's because I've changed.'

'Megan hasn't. Even as a child, she would over-think, over-plan, over-research. I guess that's part of the down side to having such a high IQ.'

'Possibly.'

'She's even making the wedding cake.'

'What? Why is she putting so much pressure on herself?'

'Because she doesn't believe anyone else could do it exactly the way it needs to be done. Besides, cooking, baking, decorating cakes — that sort of thing — relaxes her.'

'Is she doing it by herself?'

'Mum's going to help. She'll make sure Megan doesn't burn herself out too much.'

'At least your sister has someone strong to lean on.'

Jasper smiled. 'Sounds as though you like my mother.'

'I do. You're really lucky, Jasper. Many adults don't have close relationships with their parents.'

'True.'

'And she's really made me feel welcome. That's a nice feeling to have.' Jennifer smiled. 'The other day when she brought the girls round, we had a difficult time getting them out of the empty packing boxes. Isn't it amazing how much fun kids can have with an empty box?'

'The girls said they had a great time. They keep asking to come over again.'

'Oh, good. I'll let Iris know when my next day off is.'

'Unfair.'

'What?'

'I said it's unfair.'

'What is?'

'That my daughters and my mother get to spend more time with you than me.'

'That's silly. I'm with you at work all day long.'

'Yeah, on a ward round, or in theatre, or at clinic. That's hardly spending quality time together, Jen.' He raked a hand through his hair.

'We went to a concert just last night. Or did I dream that?'

'No. You most definitely didn't dream that, and neither did I.'

'I had the best time.'

'So you've said. More than once. But don't think I'm complaining. I had a great time, too.'

Jennifer found herself gazing into his eyes once more and knew she'd never grow tired of it. Things were moving fast, faster than she'd anticipated. 'Jasper, what if people at work find out we're . . . you know.'

'Interested in each other?' He laughed. 'Too late, Jen. They know.'

'What? How?'

'I think it has something to do with you calling me Jasper, rather than Eddie.'

'Really? No. I'm sure other people in the hospital call you Jasper.'

'Nope. Not one. Except for the new head of unit.'

'Oh.'

'Is that a problem? Do you think it will wreck your ice-queen status?'

'No.' She shook her head.

'Good, and for the record I just told everyone that we have mutual friends outside the hospital. That cooled the wagging tongues.'

'You did?' Jennifer sighed. 'Thank you.'

'Why? Would it be so bad for people to think that we're . . . more than colleagues? More than friends?'

'Jasper.'

Jasper shifted in his chair, glancing out to where he could see his mother spitting onto a napkin to wipe Lilly's face. He took her hand in his again, holding it tightly. 'Let me come round tonight and we can talk. Once the girls are asleep, I'll let Mum know I'll be out and she can monitor them.'

Jennifer shook her head. 'I don't think it's a good idea, Jasper.'

'Why not? We need to talk.'

'I agree with that part but . . .' She shook her head again. 'Not at my place. Just the thought of the two of us . . . alone . . . with no distractions and, well, with this . . . thing sizzling between us, it's just asking for trouble and I honestly believe it's trouble neither of us need at the moment.'

She had a point. 'Where, then? It has to be soon because I'm having trouble functioning.'

'I know. I know.' She thought. 'How about I come back to your place tonight and once the girls are in bed, we can talk? That way you don't need to bother your mother.'

'Good. I like that.'

'And I can help you get the girls ready for bed.'

Jasper was a little surprised at that. 'You really want to do that?'

'Sure. They're so yummy, Jasper. The more time I spend with them, the more I can pick up on their different personalities. I'm determined to be able to tell them apart.'

He nodded, pleased. 'They may look the same but both are unique little individuals, who usually enjoy ganging up on their father.' He smiled as he spoke and Jennifer joined in. Jasper squeezed her hand. 'I'm glad you like them.'

'I do, Jasper. You've done a brilliant job with both girls.'

'I've had help.'

'Of course, but you're their father and it's quite clear to see they love you and vice versa. It's what I always wanted with my father but . . .' She trailed off and shook her head. 'Anyway, it's nice to see.'

Jasper was now more relaxed because he was going to get to spend some time alone with her tonight. She had been right in declining to be alone at her house because he wasn't sure how much longer he'd be able to keep himself under control. The desire to touch her, to hold her close to his body, to press his lips to hers . . . everything had intensified and he'd come to the realisation that fighting what existed so naturally between them was ridiculous to ignore any more.

Lola walked into the marquee and headed straight for Jennifer, climbing up onto her knee. Surprised but delighted, Jennifer let go of Jasper's hand and put her arms around the little girl. 'How are you enjoying yourself?'

'Really good, but Uncle Matt said the sausages are almost ready but Aunty Sara said they had to cool before we ate them all.' Huffing, Lola folded her arms tightly in disgust.

'She's right, though,' Jennifer said as she watched Lilly come in and climb up onto Jasper's knee. He automatically hugged her close and pressed three quick kisses to her cheek. 'If you ate the sausage straight off the barbecue, you'd burn your tongue.' Jennifer wrinkled her nose and Lola laughed. 'That's not a nice thing to do.'

'I can blow on it,' Lola said eagerly.

'Now, that's a fantastic idea. We can cut it up for you if you like, which will help it cool faster, especially if you blow on it.'

'Will *you* cut it up for me, Jen? Please?'

'Of course.'

'I want to eat mine in the bread like a long sausage,' Lilly declared.

'So long as it's cool enough,' Jasper said, but knew Lilly had a little more patience than her sister.

Lola leaned back against her, snuggling in a little bit, and Jennifer's heart turned over with love. It hadn't taken her long to fall in love with these two adorable girls, who were so full of life, so spirited and so accepting. Jennifer glanced at Jasper as he spoke to

Lilly, smiling when he bent and blew a raspberry on Lilly's neck, making her squirm and squeal with laughter.

How long would it be, she wondered, before she fell in love with their father?

CHAPTER EIGHT

By the time they arrived back at Jasper's house, both girls were starting to get grumpy. They'd all had a fantastic afternoon, with Jennifer and Jasper receiving more than one or two meaningful looks from the family and friends around them.

'It was like being in a goldfish bowl,' Jasper joked as he carried Lilly towards her bedroom. Jennifer followed suit, Lola's arms firmly wrapped around her neck.

'I know what you mean. All eyes on us.'

'Were you wet?' Lola asked.

'Wet?' Jennifer touched her nose to the little girl's and both of them giggled. 'What do you mean?'

'Goldfish live in water,' she stated, as though it was a new scientific breakthrough. 'Were you wet?'

Both Jennifer and Jasper laughed. 'Not quite, sweetheart,' her father answered. 'Right. Time for bath.'

'No!' the girls said in unison.

'Jennifer's going to bathe you tonight and then she's going to stay for dinner and then a quick story.' Two pairs of bright blue eyes widened with delight.

'Will you check my teeth?' Lola wanted to know.

Jennifer had no idea how, exactly, she was to do this but was more than ready to agree, touched by such a request. 'I would be delighted to check your teeth.'

'Mine, too,' Lilly demanded.

'Yours too.'

'And you can have a sleepover, too.' Lilly had scrambled from her father's arms and was eagerly pulling off her clothes. 'We have a special hidey bed under my bed.' Totally naked now and without a care in the world, Lilly shifted some toys out of the way and tried to tug out the trundle bed.

'Why don't we leave the bed where it is for now and get you two into the bath?' Jasper wrapped Lilly up in a fluffy towel so she didn't get cold.

'*Please* will you sleep the night?' Lola asked, pleading and fluttering her eyelashes.

'She was born doing that,' Jasper murmured, and the adults smiled.

'I'd love to, Lola, but I have to be at the hospital bright and early tomorrow morning. Maybe another time.'

Lola opened her mouth to object but one quick look at her father had her closing it again.

'Jen will be here until you're asleep. You'll just have to be content with that.' Jasper went off to run their bath and Jennifer helped Lola undo the buttons on her dress.

'I like having you here,' Lola declared.

'Me, too,' Lilly added.

'We don't have big girls here. Sometimes Aunty Megan comes but she's been very busy with the wedding.'

'Your daddy must have lots of friends.'

'Sometimes Aunty Sara comes but mostly we go to her house.'

'You have Grandma.'

'She's not a big girl. She's an old girl,' Lola declared, little hands on her naked hips. Jennifer wrapped her in the towel Jasper had placed at the end of her bed, trying not to smile. She was discovering that four-year-olds could be very direct and brutally honest.

'Do you like my daddy?' Lilly was the one to ask the question and Jasper heard it from the hallway. He stopped just outside the door, holding his breath as he waited for Jennifer's answer.

'I do.'

'A lot?' Lola questioned.

Jennifer couldn't help but smile. 'Yes. A lot.'

'A lot, a lot?'

'Yes.' Her smile drew bigger. 'A lot, a lot.'

'Are you going to marry him?'

The smile vanished. 'Uh . . .' Jennifer was completely stunned at the question but obviously the girls were dead serious as they looked up at her with their expectant blue eyes. 'Well . . . that's an interesting ques—'

'You could be our mummy.'

'We don't have one,' Lilly added matter-of-factly, shaking her head slowly.

'Uh . . . I know.'

'She died when we was just babies but she was very pretty.'

'Like us.' Lola put her arms in the air, striking a pose and causing her towel to fall down in the process. Jennifer bent to wrap her up again.

Lilly sighed. 'I'd like a new mummy.'

'Me, too,' Lola said with an equally gorgeous sigh.

'You could live with us and have sleepovers *every* night.' Both girls agreed this was a very good plan. Jasper was still frozen to the spot outside his daughters' bedroom, unable to believe they'd voiced such a plan. Jennifer would no doubt think his children had no manners whatsoever or — worse — that he might have put them up to it.

Then he quickly reminded himself that four-year-olds had no filtering systems which, he was sure, Jennifer had already worked out. Besides, they'd managed to ask Jennifer how much she liked him and he'd been extremely pleased with the answer. The main problem he had now was to sneak away and pretend he was just coming out of the bathroom, rather than having Jennifer realise he'd been standing outside the door, eavesdropping.

'Daddy! What are you doing there?' Lilly asked as she came out of the room, almost tripping over her towel.

Jasper groaned and put a hand over his eyes. The best-laid plans . . . Scooping her into his arms, he decided the best thing was to just keep on moving rather than trying to explain. 'Bathtime, princess.' He quickly carried Lilly through and was about to go back for Lola when Jennifer carried her in.

'Princess Lola arriving for her bath,' she announced. After hanging up the towel and depositing her royal highness in the bath, Jennifer looked at Jasper. He could see in that one brief moment that she was well aware he'd overheard her conversation with the girls.

'I'll get dinner started,' he said.

'Need any help?'

'No. Stay and make sure these two mischief-makers . . .' He pointed to each child in turn causing them to giggle '. . . don't make a mess.' He gave them each a stern look before pulling a face and making them giggle once more. 'Be good for Jennifer.'

'Yes, Daddy,' they replied in that perfect unison Jennifer was now getting used to. After he'd left, she took off her jumper so she didn't get her sleeves wet and knelt down, reaching for a bath toy. Between herself and the girls they managed to make up a pretty good story, with the toys, Mr Turtle and Betsy, who was an overly large bath doll, deciding to get married. The bath book was the minister and the two plastic mermaids were the flower girls. Fifteen minutes later Jennifer looked up, surprised to see Jasper lounging in the doorway.

'How long have you been there?'

'Not long,' he answered, a large grin on his face. 'Betsy marrying Mr Turtle again?'

'Yes.'

'Third time this week.'

Jennifer stood and wiped her hands. 'You'll be very pleased to know that the flower girls walked carefully and slowly down the aisle.'

'Did they, now?' He'd seen Sara and Jennifer take the girls through their paces at the barbecue and had been very pleased with the more suitable pace. So had Megan.

'Is it time to get out, Daddy? I'm getting all wrinkly.'

'Yes, buttercup. Dinner's almost ready.' Between the two of them they managed to get the girls out, dry and dressed in their matching pink nighties in record time, and soon they were all sitting at the kitchen bench, eating chicken schnitzel and vegetables. Jennifer was impressed at how well both girls ate, not quibbling about eating the food put in front of them. Afterwards, she ended up checking two sets of teeth and reading three bedtime stories. When she'd finished, Lilly beckoned her close and put both arms around her neck, giving her a big squeezy-hug before kissing her cheek.

Lola had her turn, giving Jennifer *two* kisses. 'We like you.' She yawned as Jasper came in to kiss them and turn on their nightlight, knowing they'd be asleep within moments.

'Can I help you with the dishes?' Jennifer asked as they headed out of the girls' bedroom.

'They're all done and I'm just brewing a

pot of tea. Join me?'

'Sure.' She put her jumper back on as he took her into the lounge room. He'd straightened up the cushions and done a general tidy-up since they'd first returned.

'You've been busy.'

'I've had time. It's amazing. I was almost on the point of getting bored.'

Jennifer smiled as she sat down on the comfortable lounge, Jasper coming to sit next to her after placing the tea things down on the table. He reached for the teapot and poured them both a cup. 'I guess you're used to doing everything by yourself.'

'It's second nature.' He left his cup where it was and shifted to face her, his arm running along the back of the lounge. 'It's been nice having someone else here.'

'To help?'

'Or perhaps I should clarify that by saying it's been nice having *you* here . . . and not just because you've helped out.' He leaned forward and tucked a stray strand of hair behind her ear. Then, leaving his hand there for a moment, he looked into her eyes. They were relaxed and filled with open desire. Not only that, they were filled with acceptance and it was that acceptance that gave Jasper the confidence to follow through on his urge.

Reaching around her, he gently pulled the band from her hair and the black strands fell in a soft, silky mass around her face and shoulders. He sucked in a breath at the pretty picture. The woman was stunning. Like a child at Christmas, Jasper sifted both of his hands through the luscious locks, unable to believe how incredible they felt.

'You have the most beautiful hair.' He made sure he didn't rush, didn't tug, but instead savoured every moment of the silken strands against his skin.

'Thanks.' The word was breathless and for a second he thought he felt her tremble.

'Am I hurting you?'

'No.' She closed her eyes loving the way his fingers felt near her face, her scalp, in her hair.

'Why do you tie it back?'

She smiled as she opened her eyes. 'It gets in the way.'

'Logical . . . but why? It's perfect.' Jasper cupped her cheek and angled her head up a little. 'You're perfect.'

'No. I'm not.'

'In this moment in time, here with just the two of us, you are perfect.' He shifted to angle his body towards hers, moving in closer. They stared into each other's eyes, mentally devouring and emotionally communicating their needs. 'I want to kiss you, Jennifer.'

'Jasper.' His name was a caress and she put a hand on his chest, not to push him away but to draw him closer.

'I've been wanting to kiss you for so very long. It feels like an eternity instead of just yesterday.'

'Yes.'

'You feel it too, don't you? That amazing pull that exists between us. I know you've told me before but —'

Jennifer lifted her finger to his lips to silence him, the intimate touch sending her senses off into an anticipatory frenzy. 'You're talking far too much.'

'Mmm.' He kissed her fingertip, the sensual action making her gasp. 'I am.' He moved in closer. 'I just want to make sure . . . make sure this is what you want, too.'

'It is. I want you to kiss me, Jasper, and I wish you'd hurry up and —'

Her words were cut off as his mouth met hers, both of them sighing into the moment after that first buzz of electricity had been ignited. The tension, the build-up to that first amazing touch had been so big and so long in coming that the realisation that his mouth was actually on hers, that he could not only hold her and kiss her but that she *wanted* him to do so, was overpowering.

Jasper slid his arms around her, gathering her close. The feel of her body next to his continued to fuel his hunger but he pulled superhuman strength from somewhere to ensure he kept himself completely under control. He knew how fragile Jennifer was, what she'd been through, how big this step was for her, and he didn't want anything to ruin it.

Slowly . . . ever so slowly he moved his lips over hers, tenderly caressing and filling the emptiness she hadn't realised had been there. For a brief moment she'd been certain of feeling raw passion surge through him but in the next instant his mouth was gently exploring, gently coaxing to ensure she was right there with him, side by side on this journey into the unknown.

With a sigh of delight Jennifer lifted her hands to his head, lacing her fingers into his hair ensuring his head stayed in place. With her eyes closed, she could concentrate on the hypnotic scent of him, the pheromones which were being generated by both, mixing together with the warmth of the fire, igniting to consume them both.

Finally, the need for air made Jasper pull his mouth from hers, both out of breath.

Jennifer opened her heavy eyelids and looked at him from beneath her lashes as he placed light, feathery kisses on her cheeks, stopping in the middle to cover her lips with his as though he couldn't get enough.

'You're . . . amazing,' he whispered close to her ear, and she smiled.

'You're not so bad yourself.'

'Perhaps it's this . . . togetherness . . .' he pressed a soft kiss to her waiting lips '. . . that suits us.'

'Togetherness.' Jennifer repeated the word as though an enormous weight had been lifted from her shoulders.

Jasper eased back and looked into her eyes, smoothing his fingers through her glorious locks once more. 'I know it's not easy to take a step forward, Jen, but —

'Shh,' she whispered, and placed her finger on his lips again. 'I'm fine, Jasper. I want you to kiss me just as much as you wanted to. I wanted it last night and I wanted it now. In fact, I've been wanting it for so very long — even before you teased me by kissing my cheek the other week.' She shook her finger at him. 'And may I just say it wasn't nice to torture me like that. Sent my imagination into overdrive.'

'You and me both.' He took her finger and brought it to his lips, kissing it tenderly. Jennifer closed her eyes at the mildly erotic touch and was surprised that another wave of longing flooded through her. 'You were saying,' he murmured.

'Uh . . .' Jennifer licked her dry lips.

'Here. Let me do that for you.' The line was corny, yet perfect as he pressed his mouth to hers again, running his tongue over her lower lip, causing her to shudder with delight. Jasper accepted that shudder, taking the opportunity to enjoy the sweet sunshine that surrounded her.

When he was done, Jennifer laid her head on his shoulder and waited for her breathing to calm down. 'You're . . . potent.'

Jasper smiled at her word. 'Thank goodness you didn't say "lethal".'

Jennifer sighed and looked up at him. 'I like this.'

'This?'

'This. You and me.'

Jasper tightened his arms about her. 'Me, too.'

She giggled. 'You sound like the girls.'

'Bound to happen eventually,' he quipped. They enjoyed a few minutes' silence, both completely comfortable to just sit there and be together, absorbing the essence of each other.

'Are you comfortable?' he finally asked.

'You know, I think I am. I mean, I may have been concerned about this attraction — even a little conflicted — when it first started, but now it's different.'

Jasper's laughter rumbled joyously, surrounding them with warmth. 'That's fantastic to hear but I meant literally, not metaphorically.'

'Oh. Well, yes. I'm comfortable.' Jennifer looked up at him, her eyes intense. 'Thank you.'

'For?'

She smiled at his fishing attempt. 'For ensuring my comfort.'

'Is that all? That didn't feel like a throwaway "Thank you" to me.'

'That's because it wasn't. I guess I'm grateful that you've shown me that I can move forward with my life.' She shifted slightly, edging closer. 'That I need to reach out.' She gently urged his head towards hers. 'That I need to let go and venture out of my comfort zone. So here I go again.' At that, she pressed her mouth to his and where he'd been reining in the fire, Jennifer let it go, opening her mouth and teasing his lower lip with her tongue.

Jasper groaned and hauled her against his chest, eager to let her lead, eager to reciprocate the pace she was setting, eager to let her know he was with her all the way. 'You make my head spin,' he muttered against her mouth, both of them breathing heavily.

'Good. At least it means I'm not alone on this ride.'

'No chance of that, lady.'

'Really?' She smiled at him.

'None whatsoever. I've been fighting this attraction, trying to keep my distance, trying to give you the space I felt you needed, but now that we've passed those points, now that I've finished fighting, the only thing left for us to do is to continue moving forward.'

'To where?'

For the first time since the day had begun, Jasper heard hesitation in her voice. Was she thinking about the girls' earlier question? Did she think he wanted to marry her? He hadn't even questioned himself that far yet.

He shifted, repositioning himself on the lounge and pulling Jennifer towards him so she could rest her head more comfortably on his shoulder. As she moved, she gasped in pain, then stuck her hand down the back of the cushions and pulled out a pencil.

'Oops. Sorry. I thought I'd removed them all.'

'Never mind.' She leaned forward and put it on the table, and it was as though as she eased away from him in a physical capacity

Jasper could also feel her easing away on an emotional level, too. She picked up her teacup and took a sip, hoping the warm liquid would give her the answers to the question now flooding her mind.

'What's wrong?' he asked softly.

'What makes you think something's wrong?' She turned around so she could see him better.

'You're distancing yourself from me. Talk to me, Jen. Let me into that inner sanctum.' As he spoke, he played with the ends of her hair, still unable to stop touching her.

She liked it. The fact of the matter was, Jasper really liked her, she could see that as plain as the nose on his face, and that was fantastic. So why should she even think of hesitating?

'I don't know, Jasper.' She put her cup back on the table.

'You want this, don't you?'

'I don't know what *this* is. We're attracted to each other. We're obviously compatible when it comes to the more . . . physical aspects, but what about the girls? What about work?'

'What about work? We've covered this, Jen.'

'I know, but now it's actually happening and I can't help the way my brain freaks out. It's just how I'm wired.'

'OK.' He caressed her cheek, then leaned forward and placed a kiss on her lips. 'Thank you for letting me know.'

'Well?'

'Well, what?'

'What do we do?'

He smiled and kissed her again. 'We take it slowly. We don't flaunt it at work. We spend time together and time with the girls whenever our schedules allow. How does that sound for starters?'

Jennifer sighed and nodded. 'Good.' She paused for a moment. 'But are you sure, Jasper? Are you sure I'm what you want?'

'You're insane.' How could she *not* see just how much he wanted her?

'Possibly, but I'm also very high maintenance. I know this about myself and while it may have taken me a long time to admit it, I can do that now and I don't want my silly neuroses getting in the way of this thing between us. And even more than that, I don't want to start treating you differently at work, as though I'm trying to compensate. Neither do I want you to feel that you have to treat me any differently because, after all, let's face it, to an extent I'm your boss and that can't be easy if we're going to have disagreements about work issues.

Everything needs to be done by the book because I won't have anyone accusing me of favouritism. And as far as the girls are concerned, we'll need to be especially careful because they're so young and I love them so much and there is no way in the world I ever want to hurt them. So they'll need to be told something but I'm not at all sure what because I'm not a parent and I don't have the first idea about parenting, even though it's what I've wanted for so long, and —'

Jennifer's mouth was captured by Jasper's, effectively silencing her. When he drew back, he smiled at her. 'Would you do me the honour of accompanying me to my sister's wedding?'

'P-pardon?'

'Megan's wedding. Will you be my date?'

'Uh . . . um . . .'

Jasper smiled, causing Jennifer's stomach to flip-flop. It was amazing how the tingly tension still existed between them even after he'd kissed her the way he had. For some daft reason she'd expected it to diminish, to settle even, yet to her great astonishment it had done quite the opposite. The way he smiled seemed to affect her more than before. Perhaps it was because only a few seconds ago those very lips had been pressed to hers.

'It's not a difficult question. Or, at least, I hope it isn't.'

'I would love to go. I'd love to see the girls all done up in their pretty dresses.'

'Is that the only reason?'

'Why? Am I putting a dent in your ego?' She smiled, amazed she had such power over him.

'Yes. As a matter of fact, you are.'

'Well, then.' Jennifer touched her fingers to his cheek. 'I'd love to be your date.'

'Good.' He let out a breath.

'You were unsure?'

'Well, after you stated your . . . concerns, I wasn't one hundred per cent sure, no.'

'Sorry. I was babbling.' She shook her head, slightly embarrassed. 'I tend to do that when I'm extremely nervous but I tell you again, Jasper, I'm not an easy woman to figure out. I know my faults and I can be honest about them. I'll probably also be honest about your faults, too. I tend to freeze people out in order to protect myself from pain and hurt. See? I'm not at all easy to understand.'

'They don't call you the ice queen for nothing,' he stated with a smile. 'And you may have temporarily forgotten it but I live with two very high-maintenance females and consider myself amply qualified to take on a third. As for work, I'm sure we'll figure everything out. We have so far.'

'True.'

'We won't flaunt this relationship but I won't hide from it either. If the gossips find out, that's fine by me.' He felt her tense and cupped her face in his hands. 'It's OK, Jen. You *can* and *will* deal with it.'

'What if I freak out again?'

'Then I'll enjoy calming you down. I know how to stop you babbling, remember?' He pressed his mouth to hers and she sighed with longing.

'Seriously, Jasper. I don't like freaking out but I do. I know this about myself.'

'If you freak out, then we'll deal with it — together.'

CHAPTER NINE

During the next week, Jennifer felt like a long-tailed cat in a room full of rocking chairs — especially when she was at work. Jasper had told her they wouldn't flaunt their relationship, and they didn't, but on the first day they had to attend meetings together and she was positive that everyone in the room could see that something was definitely going on between them. At one point she even called him Eddie, rather than Jasper, to try and show that they were still only just friends. It backfired big time.

'Well, now they definitely know,' Jasper said as he fell into step with her as she headed up to her office.

'What? How?' Jennifer was so caught off guard by his comments that some of the files she was holding slipped from her grasp.

When she didn't bend down to pick them up, instead simply standing there and staring at him, Jasper bent and gathered the files. 'You called me Eddie, Jennifer. You never call me that. By doing so, you've raised suspicions. They'll all be grinning to themselves asking exactly *what* you're trying to cover up.'

'Really?'

There was such a look of wild panic in her eyes that Jasper quickly put a reassuring hand on her shoulder. 'It's all right. Remember? We said we wouldn't hide from it.'

'*You* weren't going to hide from it. I was going to run for the hills.'

'Why?' He looked a little hurt as they continued on their way and entered her office. Jasper closing the door firmly behind him. 'Why don't you want people to know?' He tried for a nonchalant pose. 'Don't think I'm good enough to thaw the ice queen?'

'Oh, Jasper. No.' She was mortified at his words and crossed to his side, taking his hands in hers, wanting to dispel the pain she saw in his eyes. 'It's not that at all. It's just different for me, that's all. They've all known you for years. I'm the new girl and head of department.'

'But we discussed this.'

'I know.' She gave his hands a little squeeze. 'I thought I'd have more time, that's all.'

'What else? Come on, Jennifer. I know you

well enough by now to sense when you're holding back.'

He was right and she was amazed at his insight. Dropping his hands, she turned and went to sit behind her desk trying to figure out how to say what she was thinking. 'It's nothing.'

'Don't go saying it's nothing because it already is. What is it?' He came around and leaned against her desk, facing her, his thigh brushing the arm of her chair. She could feel his comforting warmth enveloping her even though he wasn't touching her. Slowly, she raised her head and looked into his amazing, hypnotic eyes.

'You're the biggest catch in the hospital.'

'You make me sound like a fish.'

'You know what I mean, Jasper. You were voted most eligible Bachelor of the Hospital last year — or so Maryanne said.'

'Maryanne?'

'Yes, and she said it with a dreamy look in her eyes.'

'Nah. They were just glassy from the bug she was fighting.'

'Stop it, Jasper.' She half laughed as she spoke. 'It's easy for you to make jokes but the truth is there are plenty of women out there who, once they discover our relationship, will treat me differently. I've seen it happen before when staff date. I know of one woman who actually received anonymous hate mail because she was dating the hospital's most eligible bachelor. What if that happens to me?'

'It won't.'

'How do you know?'

'The people in Sydney aren't nearly as crazy as those who live in Melbourne.'

Jennifer shook her head and stood, moving away from him.

'I'm sorry. I'm sorry.' He came up behind her. 'I guess I'm not all that comfortable hearing you talk about me as though I'm some product on the meat market.'

'I thought you said it was fish?'

Jasper smiled and turned her round to face him, looking deeply into her eyes. 'I don't care what anyone else thinks, Jen. What's going on between us is our business and no one else's. And if anyone gives you trouble, let me know and I'll sort it out.'

'You mean, *we'll* sort it out. I don't scare that easily but I just don't want anyone else to get hurt.'

Jasper brushed a kiss across her lips. 'You are not the ice queen everyone thinks you are.'

'Found the heart beneath the ice, eh?' She

laced her hands behind his head, urging him closer.

'Absolutely.'

Thankfully, no one on the staff mentioned anything and as the day went on Jennifer began to relax a little more. She was fine when she was at home in her comfort zone or at Jasper's house. She could really let go and relax. Both Lola and Lilly were adorable and she loved spending time with them — even when Jasper was at work. On Friday, the day before Megan's wedding, Iris had been running late from an appointment with Megan and had called Jennifer to ask if she could collect the girls from day care.

'Traffic is ridiculous,' Iris said into the echoing speakerphone in her car. 'Ian's still finishing a round of golf, Jasper's working — as you know — and I didn't want to bother Sara.'

'It's fine, Iris. The day-care centre is just down the road and the girls can come back here to my place until Jasper finishes work — which is only two more hours.'

'Oh, thank you, dear. You're a lifesaver.'

'How's Megan holding up?'

'Megan's Megan. I don't know what we did to raise such a stubborn and independent woman, but that's what she is. Oh, and can you let Jasper know you've got the girls?'

'Sure. I'll call him now.'

'Thanks again. I'll see you later tonight.'

Jennifer rang off then dialled Jasper's cellphone. It was switched off. She closed her eyes and mentally recalled his timetable. Friday afternoon — he was in Theatre. Shaking her head, she opened her eyes again and dialled the hospital switch board, asking to be put through to Theatres. Hopefully, he'd be between cases or could at least let the scout nurse hold the phone for him while she spoke to him.

She was put through to Theatres, then through to the theatre Jasper was operating in.

'Hi. It's Dr Thorngate. Is, er . . . Jasper available?' Jennifer closed her eyes, hating it that she'd fumbled.

'He can't come to the phone right now, Dr Thorngate. Can I take a message?'

It was as she'd thought. There was nothing else she could do but leave a message, despite how uncomfortable it made her feel. What she could do was deliver the information in a matter-of-fact way and, hopefully, as the message was relayed to him with the entire theatre staff listening on, they wouldn't read anything . . . untoward into it.

Jennifer cleared her throat. 'Yes, you can,

221

thank you. Please let Dr Edwards know that his daughters will be at my place when he's finished work.' Jennifer bit her lip as she waited for the acknowledgement.

'Uh . . . oh. OK, then. I'll pass that message on. Thank you, Dr Thorngate.'

Jennifer returned the phone to its cradle and took a deep breath. Now it would be out. People at the hospital would now know she actually did possess a heart and it hadn't taken a supernova to thaw it — only Jasper.

She'd been gossiped about a lot in the past and had painstakingly taken steps to distance herself from recreational friendships with colleagues. She lived for her work and everyone knew that . . . but now they would know differently.

'Get a grip,' she said out loud, shaking her head as she pulled herself together. So they were going to be talking about her and Jasper. So what? She could deal with it because he was *worth* it. He'd brought so much colour into her life — as had the twins — and for the first time in years Jennifer was beginning to feel as though her heart was indeed thawing.

Collecting her keys, she drove the short distance to the daycare centre and received a warm welcome from the staff.

'Iris called through to let us know you'd be picking up the girls,' the director of the centre said after Jennifer had shown some identification. 'We'll put you on the official paperwork as a registered carer in case you need to collect them at another time.'

Jennifer's eyes widened at this news. She would now be a registered carer? Was that what she wanted? She and Jasper were dating. That was all. Wasn't it? She didn't have much time to ponder the matter as one of the girls spotted her and came running over. It was Lola and she almost knocked Jennifer to the ground as she wrapped herself around her legs.

'Jen. Jen.' Lola hugged her tightly before letting go and clapping her hands. 'Lilly!' She hollered. 'Come on.'

'I need to get my bag,' Lilly said practically, and Jennifer couldn't help but smile. That was Lil. Completely practical — like her father. From what Jasper had said about Elisha, it seemed Lola was a lot like her mother. Impulsive, direct and a little absent-minded at times.

'Get my bag, too,' Lola called.

'No.' Lilly protested, walking up while she stuffed a painting into the small bag.

'Why don't I take that for you?' Jennifer offered, smiling at the girl's determination.

'I can do it.'

Independent, determined and a little exasperating at times. Jennifer nodded. Just like her father.

Finally, the two girls were in her car, buckled safely into the back, and while they weren't sitting on their usual booster seats, it wasn't too far to drive and Jennifer knew they'd be safe.

'I love this car. It's so pretty and shiny and it smells nice.'

'Thank you.'

'I'm very excited to be going to your house, Jen.' Lola's excitement was all but bubbling over. 'I hope Daddy finishes very, very late so we have to have a sleepover.'

'But we can't because it's Aunty Megsy's wedding tomorrow and we have to get up really early and get ready,' Lilly pointed out.

'Not *that* early. Jen, can we sleep on your hiding bed? I love hiding beds. Sara has one at her house and she lets us pull it out sometimes and lie on it, but I want to sleep on one all night long.'

'Well, perhaps we can arrange it for some other time.' She was touched that Lola wanted to sleep over, knowing that Lilly would also enjoy it.

'And Daddy, too. He can sleep over, too.' Lilly added.

'But where does he sleep? He's too big for the hiding bed.' It was certainly a problem and one both girls pondered quite intently.

'He can sleep in Jen's bed,' Lilly ventured. 'That's what mummies and daddies do.' Again, Lilly's tone held that practical note.

'Oh, yeah. I forgot.'

Jennifer wasn't sure what to do or say — so she said nothing and instead concentrated on getting the girls out of the car and into the house. They continued to talk on, covering a wide variety of topics, and were more than happy to entertain each other while she prepared a snack for them.

When Jasper finally arrived the girls were lying on Jennifer's hiding bed, which she'd somehow been talked into pulling out, watching some television and relaxing.

'Sorry.' He greeted Jennifer with a kiss. That was something else she was coming to terms with as well — the fact that Jasper was intent on kissing her at every available opportunity. He was a very demonstrative man. She loved every moment of it but it still felt a little unnatural for her. 'Theatre just wouldn't end tonight.'

'Problems?'

'Mrs Verucci's total hip replacement didn't want to follow textbook procedure.'

'I hate it when they do that.' Jennifer

smiled as she spoke and was pleased when her words brought a more relaxed smile to Jasper's face. That was another thing she liked — the power she had over him. She could relax him, make him laugh, tease him, enjoy quiet moments with him. It was another world and it was a world where she didn't feel alone any more.

They ordered some food, neither feeling like cooking, and Jennifer was pleased when Jasper was talked into letting both girls have a mini-sleepover on Jen's hiding bed.

'At least I'm not the only one who's wrapped around their little fingers,' she said as she stacked the dishwasher, delighted to be able to use it. Usually, when it was just her, there was no need to put it on. She smiled, amazed at how a little domestic thing like a full dishwasher made her feel happy.

'They'll sleep in their clothes, their teeth won't be brushed and they've missed out on their bath,' Jasper pointed out as he walked over and took both of Jennifer's hands in his. 'And that's a compromise I'm willing to make if it means I get a bit of extra "grown-up" time with you.'

He bent his head and kissed her tenderly, drawing her closer into his arms. She went willingly, loving the way they fitted together.

Once the girls had fallen asleep, the two of them sat and talked quietly about books, television shows, tomorrow's wedding and work.

'Was anything said?'

'When?'

'When I left the message. Were there any . . . interested eyebrows raised?'

'I don't know. Everyone was wearing face shields and masks. A little difficult to tell.' Jasper tightened his arm around her shoulder. 'Are you expecting it?'

'When your boss calls to say that she's picking up your children and taking them back to her place, especially when it's widely known that you don't mix business and pleasure, tongues have surely got to wag.'

'And wag they will. I'm simply saying I didn't notice anything, except for extreme concentration to get Mrs Verucci's hip replacement back on track so we could all go home.' Jasper could feel her tensing up and wanted instantly to alleviate her fears. 'If we don't hide from it, then people will stop talking soon —'

'The day-care centre want to register me,' she blurted, interrupting him.

It took a second for her words to compute and it was then Jasper realised that it wasn't only the hospital situation that was bothering her. 'I think that's a good idea.'

'You do?'

'Yes. Just in case a similar thing happens in the future.'

'Oh.'

'Is that OK with you?'

'Huh? Yeah. I mean, yes. Of course it is. I mean, it's logical. Right? I live close. The girls know me. You and I often have conflicting shifts.'

'Which is something else I've been meaning to talk to you about.'

'Can we talk about it another time, please?'

Jasper could hear the hint of panic in her tone and wondered why it was there. As far as he was concerned, things were moving along beautifully between them. Sure, it was a little difficult to get some alone time but they were managing.

'Sure. Of course.'

'I just want to enjoy being with you.' She pulled his arms about her and snuggled into him. She looked over to the sofa bed opposite where they sat, her heart warming at the sight of the sleeping twins.

'You'll get no argument from me.' He wanted to hold her for ever and he also wanted to let her know that he was definitely in love with her. He wasn't exactly sure when it had happened but it had. The fact that it had was a miracle in itself as after Elisha's death he'd been certain he'd never love again. He also knew that confessing this to Jennifer would freak her out even more and that was the last thing he wanted. Slow and steady won the race. That's what he'd learned as a child and that was the tactic he was employing right now because he had to do whatever it took to convince Jennifer that they belonged together. The four of them. Together. A family.

'Why are we getting back into the car, Daddy?' Lola wanted to know. 'We haven't walked down the aisle yet.'

'The church is really pretty and I love the flowers.' Lilly spoke as Jennifer helped her into the car and started to do up her seat belt.

'I love the flowers, too.' Lola's tone was wistful.

'And we promise to walk really slowly, Daddy,' Lilly continued. 'Just like Jen showed us. Nice and slow.'

'We won't run. Honest, we won't.' Lola's eyes were earnest.

Jasper looked across at Jennifer and together they had a flash of clarity.

'You know this isn't your fault,' Jennifer

quickly reassured both girls, and Jasper agreed with her. Although how he was going to explain that Aunty Megan wouldn't be getting married today because her creep of a fiancé had left her stranded at the altar, he had no idea.

Both girls opened their mouths to talk but Jasper got there first. 'Shh. Just for a moment, please,' he instructed his daughters. 'Listen to Daddy.' He leaned further into the car and kissed each one on the cheek. 'I am so proud of both of you. You've been very well behaved.'

'And we didn't get our dresses messy.'

'I know, but unfortunately there isn't going to be a wedding today.'

'But we'll walk slo—'

'Shh,' he said softly, and placed his finger on Lola's little lips. 'Aunty Megan is very sad and upset because Calvin has changed his mind.' Two pairs of bright blue eyes looked back at him. Jasper glanced at Jennifer who nodded encouragingly for him to continue. 'Calvin doesn't want to marry Aunty Megan.'

'Well, that's just dumb,' Lola mumbled against his finger. Jasper smiled and kissed her head.

'I couldn't agree more, pumpkin, but that's the reason you don't get to walk down the aisle. It's not your fault. Either of you. You're not being punished. Understand?'

'We're *all* proud of you,' Jennifer reiterated.

'Grandma and Grandpa?'

'Yes.'

'Sara and Matt?'

'Yes. *All* of us,' Jasper emphasised. 'Now, if you could just sit in the car for a few more minutes, Jen and I are going to check with Grandpa that everything else is under control. Can you both sit quietly?'

'Yes, Daddy,' they said in unison.

'Excellent. We'll head home soon.'

'There's no party?' Lola wasn't happy about that.

'Aunty Megan said there would be a party afterwards.' Lilly nodded her head enthusiastically, trying to convince her father.

Jasper shook his head sadly. 'Sorry, girls. No party. We'll be back in a moment.' He put the window down a bit, then shut the car door, waiting for Jen to follow suit before they walked over to where his father was standing outside of the church, talking to Sara.

'How's Megan?' Jasper asked his father.

'Not crying.' Ian shook his head. 'Stubborn as a mule, that one. That's the Irish in the family coming out, I'm afraid.'

'I still can't believe Calvin stood her up.' Jasper ground his teeth together and clenched his fists. A moment later he felt Jennifer's hand cover his, gently prising his fingers open so she could hold his hand. Jasper looked down at her as his father agreed with the sentiment, generally berating his ex-son-in-law-to-be, but Jasper didn't hear. When he'd looked down at Jennifer, to see such calm reassurance in her eyes, he somehow knew things were going to be all right. It was a strange sensation and one he'd never felt before. This woman simply exuded strength and power and he knew it was because she had gone through so much herself. His love for her increased even more and he gave her a little smile of thanks.

Jennifer gazed up at him, so happy she could be there to help him out. In fact, she wanted to keep helping him out for the rest of his life. She wanted to be there for him, for the girls. She wanted to be a part of them for ever and she looked away, starting to tremble inside. The thought of another woman helping Jasper and the girls through such a deeply personal time like this made her feel sick to her stomach.

The last time she'd had these sorts of symptoms, she'd diagnosed herself to be in love. This time was no different. She was completely and utterly in love with Jasper Edwards.

CHAPTER TEN

'What a horrible day for Megan.' Jasper kept his voice low as they drove along. The girls had some of their favourite music playing in the back and were happily singing along so there was no way they could overhear the conversation in the front.

'Mmm.' Jennifer looked down at her clenched hands, still trying to come to terms with her most recent discovery. She was in love with Jasper? How on earth had that happened? She was desperately trying to rake through the memories from the time they'd met until now to see if she could pinpoint the exact moment it had happened, but she couldn't. It was simply that the more she saw of Jasper and his daughters, the more she wanted to be with all of them. She wanted to go to work in the morning and know they would be waiting when she got home. She wanted to cut down on her shifts to spend more time with the girls. She wanted to take the girls to the park with Jasper on a day off where they would all walk hand in hand, where she would push the girls on the swing, where she would catch them at the bottom of the slippery-dip, where she would be able to look up into Jasper's smiling face and see the love in his eyes . . . the love he would have for her.

Jennifer swallowed over the sudden dryness in her throat. Was it possible that Jasper would ever risk his heart again? Ever marry again? He seemed more than content with his sectioned-off life of family and work, throwing in the occasional date with a pretty colleague so he didn't get bored. Was that how he wanted things to continue? Was that what he wanted for them? For her to be the person he took to functions, who he spent time with but who he wasn't ready to really commit to?

'Are you all right?' Jasper asked softly, and Jennifer quickly looked up to reassure him. That was a mistake in itself. His eyes were so rich, so deep, so unbelievably sexy that she couldn't hide the tremor of excitement that coursed through her.

'Jen?' His voice dropped lower when he said her name like that and she could read his instant desire for her. It was utterly amazing how they seemed to be able to set each other off with just a look and she was glad that at least that part of the relationship was intensely reciprocated. 'What is it?' He glanced at her, trying to decipher her expression before looking back at the road.

Jennifer opened her mouth to speak but found herself incapable of forming a sentence. It was on the tip of her tongue to simply blurt out her true feelings, to tell Jasper that she'd just realised she was in love with him, but she knew she couldn't. She didn't want to wreck what was happening between them and, besides, she needed to think this through. Her head had been quite fuzzy of late and she'd been experiencing a general feeling of exhaustion at the end of the day, more so than usual, and now she knew what the diagnosis was — she was in love.

His gaze flicked to her one more time before he slammed on the brakes and gripped the steering-wheel tightly. Jennifer instinctively put her hand out to the dashboard but the seat belt held her in. The car skidded forward, heading towards the stationary block of cars in front of them which had already crashed.

Jennifer closed her eyes for a second, waiting for that sickening sound of metal, twisting with metal but it never came. Everything had happened so fast and, thankfully, Jasper had brought his own car to a stop within a reasonable distance. He checked his rear-view mirror to find the car behind him had already stopped as well before he turned to check on his girls.

'Jen? You OK?'

'Yes.'

'Girls?'

'Daddy?' Lilly's lower lip was starting to wobble.

'Daddy?' Lola echoed, her eyes wide with fright.

'It's OK, girls. We're all all right. There's been an accident up ahead. I'm just going to have a look.' Jasper was out of the car before they knew what was happening. Jennifer undid her own seat belt before wriggling herself into the back seat and placing an arm about both girls as they started to cry.

'It's all right,' she comforted them. 'It's over. We're all OK.'

'I want to get out,' Lola protested, tugging on her seat belt.

'No, no, darling. Just wait a moment. Let me check you both.' Jennifer was visually giving them a once-over, only breathing out a sigh of relief when she'd reassured herself they were indeed both all right. Her cell-phone began to ring, which momentarily stopped the girls from crying, and Jennifer quickly reached into the front seat to answer it.

'Jen? It's Sara. Are you all right?'

'We're fine. Where are you?'

'About five cars back.'

'Great.' Jennifer looked out the window to see that several motorists had stopped their cars blocking off the lane next to the crash, and were directing traffic. 'Why don't you come and get the girls and take them to your house? I have a feeling Jasper and I will be in Theatre for a few hours.'

'Of course. Be right there.'

It didn't take much to pack up the girls who were both more than happy to go with Sara in her mini-van. Jennifer and Jasper kissed them both goodbye and once they were gone Jasper took her hand in his as they walked back towards his car.

'The emergency services have already been called and I just need to get my medical kit from the car. Although there are several cars involved in the pile-up, the worst seems to be the motorcyclist at the front. He obviously had to brake hard and then went not only over his own handlebars but over the car in front which I believe was the one that caused the accident in the first place.'

'I'll take the cyclist. You do a closer triage on the other vehicles then report back and help me.'

Jasper couldn't help the smile that touched the corners of his mouth. 'Yes, boss,' he said, and laughed away Jennifer's brief look of alarm.

'Sorry. I guess it's just habit.'

'And one that suits you.' They were at his car now and before Jasper opened the boot to retrieve his medical bag he bent his head and placed a firm kiss to Jennifer's lips.

Wishing she had a change of shoes, Jennifer made her way in her high heels towards the motorcyclist. There was a man sitting beside him, talking to him, keeping him alert. The rider still had his helmet on and she was thankful no one had tried to remove it.

'Hi. I'm Dr Thorngate.' She knelt down as best she could, given the tightness of the dress she was wearing, and was momentarily thankful she'd gone for the rich, deep burgundy colour as it wouldn't show many of the stains she knew the garment was about to get.

'You're a doctor?' The man sitting beside the rider sounded doubtful. 'You don't look like one.'

'Well, I could hardly wear my operating clothes to a wedding, now, could I?' She opened the medical kit Jasper had given her and pulled on a pair of gloves as she did a visual assessment of the injured man, thankful he was still conscious. His upper torso was angled slightly but appeared fine. It was his left leg, twisted in an odd way, that gave her the most concern.

'What's your name?' she asked him.

'Hamish.'

'All right, Hamish. I want you to keep as still as you can, especially your head, but can you tell me where it hurts the most?'

'My lower back. My leg.' Hamish lifted his right hand to try and indicate the areas but she quickly put her hand on his.

'Stay still,' she reminded him. 'I'm going to look at your leg now. I need to check to make sure I can feel the pulse there.' She shifted down and pressed her fingers to the posterial tibial pulse but couldn't feel anything. She then checked his popliteal and femoral pulses and was pleased to find the femoral one quite strong. The main break appeared to be around the knee and lower leg. 'I need to move your leg, Hamish, in order to get some more blood flowing. I'm going to give you something for the pain. Are you allergic to anything?'

'Not that I know of.'

'Good.' Jennifer drew up an injection and administered it, then looked up to see Jasper heading her way. 'How are things going?' she asked as he reached out a hand to help her to her feet.

'I guess you're not really dressed for this, are you?' His gaze once again flicked briefly over her body, his reaction even more intense than the first time he'd seen her dressed like this earlier on in the day.

'Neither are you.' She indicated his suit. 'But at least you're more comfortable.' She indicated the destruction behind him. 'What's the verdict?' The sounds of a siren in the distance pierced the air.

'A lot of whiplash, a lot of bruises.' He shrugged. 'A lot of angry and upset people. Nothing major.'

'Good. As soon as the paramedics get here, I want to get a cervical collar onto Hamish and then we can deal with him at the hospital. His left leg will require surgery so if I could borrow your phone, I'll call it through to see if I can secure an emergency theatre.'

Jasper handed over his phone immediately. 'You know, Jen, there are other people who work at the hospital. They're there now, covering the accidents that come in. You are allowed to have time off.'

Jennifer merely nodded before speaking into the phone. Jasper bent down and continued treating Hamish, straightening out his leg to allow stronger blood flow to the fractured limbs. When the ambulances arrived, Jennifer travelled with Hamish while Jasper managed to drive his car out and follow them to the hospital.

'Get him directly into X-ray,' she told Maryanne, who greeted them there. 'Jasper, you're with me.' With that, she headed directly to the female changing rooms and started to peel off her dress. She stopped, arms raised, as she caught a glimpse of herself in the mirror. Slowly she lowered her hands and took a moment to simply look. She'd been surprised when Iris had insisted on taking her shopping for a dress to wear to the wedding.

'You've been working too hard, Jennifer,' Iris had scolded as they'd tripped from one dress shop to the next. Sara had managed to meet them and after a quick lunch, the hunt for the perfect dress had continued.

'You need to take a break,' Sara had reiterated and had then gasped with glee as she'd discovered the very dress that Jennifer was now wearing. 'Wear your hair up, with a few little white flowers.'

'Flowers?' Jennifer had raised her eyebrows in disbelief.

'Oh, yes,' Iris had gasped. 'They'd look beautiful with your dark locks.'

'Jasper will go wild.' Both Iris and Sara had giggled like schoolgirls at this idea. 'I'll come around beforehand and do it for you . . . and your make-up.'

'He won't know what hit him.' Iris had hugged Jennifer close.

Before Jennifer had been able to reply, Sara had insisted on paying for the dress and had then led them on the search for the necessary accessories.

And poor Jasper *hadn't* known what had hit him when he'd opened his front door and seen her standing there. She knew this because he'd been unable to speak as his gaze had covered every inch of the vision before him. Then he'd taken her hands in his and carefully leaned down to kiss her lips. It had been one of the most romantic moments she'd ever experienced. The memory filled her heart with love for the man who was no doubt waiting for her to change so they could perform surgery on poor Hamish.

It was true what Jasper had said. There were other people who could do this operation and Hamish's injuries were hardly life threatening. Instead, they could have just let the paramedics deal with the situation and left to return to the girls.

But would the girls be waiting for *her?* Or were they just waiting for their father to return? Again Jennifer was struck with the thought that she really had no idea of the part she played in this family's life. Was she a necessary part? Was she superfluous? Was she simply a novelty which would wear off later?

The desire to be with them all — including the extended family of Iris and Ian — was overwhelming and for the first time in her life she desperately wanted to be needed. Sitting down on a nearby chair, she realised she was shaking and knew if she didn't pull herself together she wouldn't be able to perform any surgery, even if she wanted to.

A wave of tiredness swamped her. Tiredness from working herself so hard, of always needing to push, to work her way to the top. It was then, and only then, she acknowledged she hadn't really stopped for the past eight years — not since Arturo's death.

She'd used work as a means of getting through her grief and in the process she'd lost herself . . . until she'd met Jasper. Another wave of fatigue washed over her.

This time her stomach began to churn and she realised she probably should eat something.

At the knock on the change-room doors, Jennifer looked up, then stood up. Before she could take a step, she could hear the beeping of the combination buttons being pressed and a second later the door clicked open.

'Jennifer?'

It was Jasper.

'Jen? Are you all right?'

She walked out to where he could see her and when he saw she was still in her incredible dress, he smiled. 'Need some help with the zip?'

Jennifer shook her head, then wished she hadn't as the room started to spin. She wasn't sure whether she actually said something or whether Jasper had been watching her closely, but in the next instant he was beside her and holding her firmly in his arms.

'I've got you. I've got you. Here, sit down.' He led her back to the chair and forced her to sit. He pressed a hand to her forehead. 'You're warm. Do you feel sick?'

'I'll be fine.' But even as she heard herself speak, her throat dry, her voice cracking on the last word, Jennifer realised she wasn't at all fine.

'What happened? It's only been five minutes since I left you.'

She looked up at him and was surprised to see two images of him swimming before her eyes. 'I stopped.'

'Stopped what?'

'I stopped. I've been going . . .' she panted '. . . for so long. I've been in survival mode for eight years and just, well . . . I just . . . I *stopped.*' She tried to shake her head again but the nausea which rose up was worse than before.

'Right. That's it. I'm getting you home.'

'No.'

'Yes.' His tone was firm and brooked no argument. 'You're not well, Jen, and you're exhibiting symptoms of the dreaded lurgy that has been sweeping its way through the hospital.'

'Don't come close.' Even she couldn't believe how bad she felt, but the last thing she wanted was for Jasper to get it from her.

'You've got Buckley's and no hope of that happening.'

'You'll get it.'

'I have a strong constitution. Comes from hanging around with preschoolers.'

She could tell he was smiling as he helped

her up. 'I like it when you smile.' The words were said softly as she leaned in to him. 'I like the way you smell. Always nice.'

'Good to know.' Jasper tried to put her arm around his neck so he could support her as they walked out but realised that all of her strength had gone and she was definitely coming down with whatever it was. 'Hold on, honey.' He pressed a kiss to her forehead and realised her temperature was raised. 'I've got you.' With that, he swept her off her feet and carried her towards the door. She was lighter than he'd expected and thankfully he was able to navigate his way out of the female changing rooms with the orthopaedic head of unit cradled safely in his arms.

Jennifer wasn't aware of much except that Jasper stopped to talk to someone. It might have been Maryanne, she couldn't remember. Everything became fuzzy, taking on a dream-like haze, and before she knew it she was lying in her bed and someone was taking off her shoes.

'Jasper?'

'I'm here, Jen. Still here. Not going anywhere. Sit up, honey. I need you to swallow some tablets.'

'No.' Her head was heavy and her limbs felt like lead.

'It's just paracetamol. It'll help. Trust me.'

'Trust you?' Jennifer opened her bleary eyes and looked at him. 'I do. I trust you, Jasper. I love you, Jasper.' She dutifully swallowed the tablets and after that all she remembered was closing her eyes and letting the sweet darkness of rest consume her.

Jasper stood and stared down at her. His Jennifer. The woman who'd just admitted to not only trusting him but to loving him. Was this real? Was this true? He hoped it was. He hoped so with all his heart.

Right now, though, she needed him and there was no way on this earth that he was going to let her down. Knowing his parents had enough to deal with in supporting Megan, he called Sara to let her know what the situation was.

'Of course I'll keep the girls overnight. They're fine. Don't worry about them. Perhaps having a sleepover will make up for the fact that they didn't get to walk down the aisle today. They've still been practising.'

'Oh, my crazy, darling daughters.' Jasper couldn't help but smile at this news.

'You just take care of Jen. She needs you, Jasper.'

'I know.' He nodded as he looked towards her bedroom. 'And I need her just as much.'

Jennifer woke with a start. She was positive she'd slept through her alarm, that she was late for work. Was it her first day on the job? No. She'd been back in Parramatta for some time now. She frowned and went to lift the covers off her body and discovered it was almost impossible to move. Everything ached. She lay still, trying to remember. Had she been in an accident? Was she in hospital?

She slowly opened her eyes and looked around. She was in her own room. She relaxed a little and lay silently for a moment, desperately trying to remember. It was then she realised she wasn't alone, the breathing of someone next to her almost echoing around the room. Her heart thudded wildly as she forced herself to move and was momentarily surprised at seeing Jasper lying next to her . . . still dressed in the trousers and shirt he'd worn to his sister's non-wedding.

And then she remembered. She was sick. She never got sick but here she was — sick — and Jasper had taken care of her. There was a weight around her waist and she realised he had his arm over her, and although she was beneath the covers and he was on top with a blanket half over him, she'd still somehow snuggled up to him as they'd slept.

'Hi.'

Jennifer's gaze flicked up to meet his. He hadn't moved but his eyes were open and his lips were curved into a caring smile.

'How are you feeling? Any better?'

Jennifer opened her mouth to talk but coughed instead. Turning her face away into the pillow, she moaned.

'That good, eh?' Jasper chuckled and lifted his arm as he sat up. Jennifer felt instantly bereft at his departure. 'Let's get some more paracetamol into you.' He checked his watch. 'Yep, you're about due for another dose.'

It was then she remembered him waking her up every four hours and making her swallow pills. She remembered him sponging her forehead with cool, refreshing water and also taking her temperature. When he returned, she didn't speak until after she'd taken the pills.

'Thank you.'

'For?'

'Staying.'

Jasper sat on the bed beside her and brushed a strand of hair away from her face

— her glorious hair which now bounced around her face and shoulders. 'How could I not stay when you begged me so charmingly not to leave you?'

'Did I?' Jennifer closed her eyes as she recalled holding his hand against her cheek and asking him not to go. 'Oh, I did.' She groaned and sunk deeper into the pillows.

Jasper laughed again. 'Don't worry, Jen. I wasn't going anywhere.'

'The girls.' Her eyes snapped open.

'They're fine. They're with Sara. And if you'd like a further update, when I called to check on them earlier, they were busy making bread rolls and planning to make Sara's boys marry them later on *just* so they could walk down an imaginary aisle.'

Jennifer tried to laugh but every muscle in her body seemed to scream with agony. Added to that, she ended up coughing.

'Rest.' Jasper once more came forward to kiss her but she pushed him away. 'Ah . . . that doesn't work, Jen.'

'You'll get sick,' she said between coughs.

'No, I won't. In fact, in kissing you, I might just be passing on some good antibodies to help fight the good fight.'

'That's rubbish.'

'I know, but I'm the doctor and you're the patient and what I say goes.' He stood, leaned over her and kissed her full on the mouth. 'Now rest.'

And that was how the day progressed with Jennifer sleeping most of it away while Jasper took care of her. It was close to eight o'clock on Sunday evening when she started feeling as though she had a little more energy.

It was then she was able to fully comprehend that Jasper had not only taken out her intricate hairstyle but had removed her clothes. It was true that she was wearing a red nightshirt he'd obviously found in one of her drawers and she was pleased he'd not left her to sleep just in her underwear. Still, the realisation that Jasper had undressed her was one that warmed her cheeks.

'Your temperature is still slightly elevated,' he said.

'Uh . . . that's actually got nothing to do with the lurgy and everything to do with my embarrassment.'

'Embarrassment? Whatever for?'

'Well, I don't remember getting changed.'

'Ah.' Jasper nodded slowly. 'No need to worry. I'm a doctor. Completely professional. You were fine — er . . . I mean, *it* was fine.' He stopped, his smile wide and, oh, so sexy. 'Either way, I couldn't let you ruin your beautiful dress.'

'Well . . . thank you.'

'You are most welcome, my gorgeous Jennifer.'

'Gorgeous?'

'Fishing?'

'No. I just don't think I look all that gorgeous at the moment.'

'Well, you do, and as I'm the one who has to look at you, my opinion is all that counts. Here.' He held out a large piece of cardboard which had been folded in half to make a card. 'This is for you from the girls.'

'Oh. Are they all right? What about your parents? Megan? How is she? Oh, and that young man, the cyclist? How did his surgery go?'

Jasper came around the bed and lay down next to her, carefully pulling her into his arms. 'Right. Well, let's see. The girls are fine. They came over earlier but you were asleep and I've not long got back from tucking them into their beds and kissing them goodnight.'

'But what if they —'

'Shh. They've both had this bug so they'll be fine. Now, where was I? Oh, yes. The girls are fine, my parents are fine as well and send their best regards for a speedy recovery. Megan is . . . well, apparently she still hasn't cried a single tear but I guess that's just

Megan. And the young cyclist — Hamish — has been taken out of HDU and is now on the general ward, recovering nicely. Now, open your card and marvel at the talent of my girls.'

Jennifer shifted, snuggling in closer to him as she dutifully read the card which contained drawings from both girls.

'They're wonderful, Jasper. I love them so much.' She held the card close to her chest.

'I'm glad to hear that.'

'Mmm. You feel nice.'

'Don't go to sleep just yet. You need to have another lot of tablets in about fifteen minutes.'

'Oh? OK.' She didn't open her eyes and her body relaxed against him. 'Why are you so good to me, Jasper?'

'Because I'm in love with you.'

CHAPTER ELEVEN

The words were spoken with heartfelt conviction and Jennifer sighed longingly as she drifted off into the most peaceful sleep she'd had in almost a decade.

'Jen?' Jasper tried to shift a little so he could see she'd heard him. 'Jennifer?' Her eyes were closed and her breathing was deep and relaxed. Jasper shook his head, unable to believe his bad luck. The moment he confessed his true feelings . . . she slept.

Jasper stayed for a while longer, deciding he wouldn't wake her up to take her tablets but instead leave a glass of water by the bed with the medication next to them so she didn't need to get out of bed.

He stood there for the umpteenth time, looking down at this amazing woman, and again he found it impossible not to reach out and run his fingers through her hair. Why she kept it pulled back into that tight bun he couldn't fathom because she was absolutely stunning with it flowing in dark, wavy locks around her face.

He knew she still had things to work out, knew he probably shouldn't have even mentioned the word 'love' tonight, but his feelings for her were becoming increasingly difficult to repress. Kissing her forehead, he left her room and made sure the rest of her house was tidy. There were still one or two boxes left to unpack and although she'd put them out of the way, when the girls had been over earlier in the day, they'd started pulling some of Jennifer's things out, intent on climbing into the empty box and having a grand old time. Jasper had stopped them and packed everything back.

That's when he'd found the photo album and he hadn't been able to resist looking through it.

The album contained pictures of a much younger Jennifer. Her hair had been a lot shorter back then, which surprised him, but she still looked amazing. He came across photographs of a much younger looking Sara as well. There was a sombre photograph of her father in full military uniform with his wife dutifully at his side. And then the photos of Jennifer and the man he could only assume was Arturo. He had a love of life in his eyes which even the picture had captured perfectly.

Jasper turned the page and came across a photograph of Jennifer with her arms around Arturo and could see just how happy she'd been back then. He didn't feel the remotest hint of jealousy, which surprised him. He'd been jealous when her young patient, Christopher, had made her laugh, but not now when he was looking at Jennifer's past. Instead, he felt an overwhelming sense of sadness at all she'd lost. He understood this sadness because he'd lost so much as well.

He put the album down, closing it carefully and running his hand over the textured front cover. He had his own albums, his own memories of his past, but that's exactly what they were now . . . memories of the past. His girls had helped him to remain firmly in the present and that had helped him look forward to a new future.

A lone tear slid down Jasper's cheek as he not only felt the loss of Elisha but the loss Jennifer had obviously felt after Arturo's death. It was a bond which had brought them together, a bond which had helped them to move to the next stage of their lives. He'd loved and lost once and he wasn't going to do it again. Jennifer was far too important to his happiness, to the girls' happiness, and he was determined to convince his boss they not only belonged together but that there was no need to feel guilty any more because she'd gone on living.

He had a future waiting for him. A future he wanted with Jen.

When Jennifer awoke the next morning, she was a little disappointed not to find Jasper lying next to her. Perhaps he was already up. She checked the clock, moaning a little when her muscles protested. It was only just after six o'clock.

'Jas—' She stopped, coughing on the words, her throat dry. She smiled as she saw the tablets and water he'd left for her, a little sticky note attached to the glass which said, 'Swallow the tablets and don't argue with your doctor.' He'd also added a big, bold 'X' beneath it which made her smile widen. 'Jasper?' she called, but received no answer. She tried again but there was only silence as an answer.

He'd obviously left and she knew he had every right to. He had other priorities, other people who needed him more than she did, and she understood this completely. So why did tears suddenly spring to her eyes and why did she feel so bereft without him?

'Because you love him, you ninny,' she

whispered. She snuggled back into the covers for a moment, then thought better of it. She wasn't the type to simply lie there and wallow in her own misery and all because Jasper had gone home to look after his daughters. No. She was a determined woman and one who had fended for herself for most of her life.

Flicking back the covers, she took her time getting out of bed and, moving slowly, shuffled off towards the bathroom.

By the time Jasper unlocked her front door just after half past seven, Jennifer was showered and dressed and sitting at the kitchen table, enjoying a very light breakfast.

'Well. Look at you.' Jasper's eyes widened at the sight of her, thankful that she'd left her hair loose. 'You're looking much better.' He enveloped her in his arms, stroking her hair and kissing her forehead. 'Temperature is right down.' He pulled back slightly to look into her eyes. 'Eyes have lost their glassy look. You're still a bit congested, but that's to be expected.' He brushed a warm and inviting kiss across her lips. 'Lips appear to be in working order and tasting of peppermint tea and . . . Is that strawberry jam?' He dipped his head for another kiss, this one slightly longer than the last. 'Yep.'

He smacked his own lips together. 'Definitely strawberry.'

'There's more tea in the pot if you'd like a cup.'

'I've just had some coffee.' He released her and sat down next to her.

'How are the girls?'

'Eager to come down and see you. I told them I had to make sure you were awake but if you're feeling up to it, Mum will bring them down later for a fifteen-minute visit. No more than that because they'll tire you out too quickly and the last thing you want is a relapse.'

'True.' She ran her hand lovingly down his tie. 'Off to work?'

'Someone's got to keep the department running. I'll make your excuses for the meetings and, thankfully, as all the rest of your staff have had this bug and are now back at work, clinic shouldn't be too hectic.'

'I could probably go to the meetings,' she suggested, but he vetoed that idea immediately.

'You're on sick leave, Dr Thorngate. Now, do as you're told.'

'And what's my prescription?' She winked at him as she said the words and Jasper's eyes widened in delighted surprise.

'You *are* feeling better. Good to see.'

'I thought I must be getting better, otherwise you would have stayed last night.'

He could see the longing in her eyes, see the need she had for him, and his heart overflowed with love. 'I wanted to.' Jasper took her hand in his. 'It was almost impossible to drag myself out of here but the gir—'

'Shh.' She placed a finger on his lips. 'You don't need to explain. I just missed you, that's all.'

'Really?' He kissed her finger, then took both her hands in his. 'I missed you, too.'

'That's nice.'

'It is.' Jasper once more looked over at the photo album then back to Jennifer. He could simply sit there and look into her eyes all day long, which was exactly what he wanted to do right now but he knew he couldn't. 'I hope you don't mind but I had a look through your photos.' He pointed to the album.

'My photos?'

'I wasn't snooping when I found it,' he added quickly and told her how the girls had 'helped' unpack so they could play in the boxes.

'It's OK, Jasper.' Her smile was welcoming as she caressed his cheek. 'I don't mind.' She let go of one of his hands and picked up the album, looking at the outside for a long moment before speaking. 'I used to look at this album every night for so long. Just touching the photographs of Art used to make me feel closer to him somehow.'

Jasper only nodded and although she'd felt silly saying those words, she knew he would understand completely.

'People always say the first year after losing someone is the hardest, and it was. It was a really difficult year for me but looking at our memories, at the good times we'd shared, really helped to get me through.' Jennifer sighed. 'The memories are a part of me, just as Art will always be a part of me.'

She paused and breathed in deeply before continuing. 'There's a park — not far from here — where we used to go to just sit and watch the world. Kids would play. Birds would chirp. Leaves would fall. Clouds would float by. It was one of my favourite places and Art would lie on the grass and tell me about his day, about the children he'd taught and how we'd have our own brood someday. It was . . . nothing, you know. We talked about nothing yet all those nothings came to mean . . .'

'Everything.' Jasper's tone was soft and he squeezed her hand. 'It's the little things, the quiet moments, you tend to remember the most.'

'Yes.' Jennifer smiled a watery smile at Jasper.

'I used to watch the girls do something new and exciting, like feeding themselves for the first time or talking or running or jumping or doing a sommersault. Little, everyday things, and I'd be almost mad at Elisha for missing it, for not being there to share in those all important moments.'

'Yes. I'd get mad at Art for not being there and then I'd feel guilty for feeling that way.'

Jasper shook his head. 'No need to feel guilty. The anger is a part of the grieving process.'

'I know. Even though I didn't go to counselling, I did read a few books on the subject.'

He smiled at that. 'Me, too. Anyway, about a year ago Lilly caught a ball for the first time. She was so happy, so excited, especially with her little tongue between her teeth as she concentrated so hard on keeping her hands together, ready to accept the ball. It was then I started to think, Elisha would have loved that. Instead of, She's missing it, my thoughts somehow turned themselves around to think, She'd have loved that, and she would have. She'd have been so proud of our Lilly.'

'Yes.' His words made perfect sense and she nodded. 'I do understand that.' She leaned forward and brushed a kiss across his lips. 'Thank you for listening to me, for sharing with me.'

'You're more than welcome, my beautiful Jen, but there's also something else I want to say. It may not be easy for you to hear it but I need to say it.' He paused, took a deep breath and then said carefully, 'You need to say goodbye to him, Jen.' The words were spoken so quietly that hardly any sound came out from between his lips but Jennifer felt his words and knew he was right.

'Did you say goodbye to Elisha?'

'Yes. At one of Sydney's most prestigious restaurants, because that was where we had our first date and also where I proposed, so it seemed only right to say goodbye there, too.'

Jennifer looked down at the hand he held before meeting his eyes once more. 'Was it difficult?'

'Yes. I sat in that restaurant, by myself, surrounded by couples, and realised that I was now on my own. *Really* on my own. She wasn't in the bathroom or at the shops or outworking. She was gone and she was gone for ever. After that night, somehow, I was able to move on. I was able to come home from work and not expect her to be there, waiting for me. I was able to start living again.' He let go of her hand to cup her face. 'And if I hadn't started living again, I wouldn't have met you.'

The kiss he pressed to her lips was full of promise, full of hope and most of all full of love. Jennifer leaned back and looked at him, her brain fuzzy from the past few days, filtering something important through it.

'Did you tell me last night that you loved me?' she blurted out, and immediately wished she hadn't. What if he hadn't? What if she'd simply dreamt that part and Jasper wasn't at all in love with her? Holding her breath, she waited for his reaction and almost collapsed with relief when his lips twitched into a smile.

'I did and you promptly fell asleep.'

'Oh. Sorry. I was tired.'

'I know.' He kissed her. 'Not the most flattering response, I must say.'

Jennifer giggled. 'Must have brought your ego down a notch or two.'

'My ego — thank you very much — is just fine and, I'd like to point out, hardly ever elevated or puffed up.'

Jennifer only laughed again.

'Do you mind?' he asked softly, all traces

of humour vanishing.

'About?'

'About me loving you.' He said the words as though he was unsure of her reception of them.

'Oh, Jasper.' Jennifer laced her fingers through his hair, urging his head down so she could show him just how much she *didn't* mind. The kiss was long and slow and he was sure, filled with as much love for him as he had for her . . . but she still didn't say the words. Perhaps she couldn't . . . not until she'd said her goodbyes to her past love.

When they pulled back, both slightly breathless, he rested his forehead against hers. 'I have to go. Duty calls but I'll try and get away earlier from clinic so we can go this afternoon.'

'Go? Go where?'

'To your park.'

Jennifer watched as he straightened his jacket and took his car keys from his pocket. He was an amazing man, patient, understanding and loving. He was helping her to move on with her life because he understood exactly what it was like. He'd been there and he'd safely traversed the pit of despair to come out the other side.

She had listened to what he'd said and

known instantly that he was right but did they have to go so soon? This afternoon? To *the* park? She could see the determined look in Jasper's eyes as though he knew exactly what she was thinking. If she prolonged saying goodbye to Art, who knew what she'd miss in the meantime? No. Jasper was right. It had to be this afternoon. It had to be today because she didn't want to miss one more second of her new life with this man who loved her.

Slowly she nodded. 'We can go in Miss Chief. The girls love that car as much as I do.'

He pressed his lips to hers again before heading to the door. 'You've got yourself a date, Dr Thorngate.'

The park was the same. Exactly the same. Of course, the trees and shrubs were taller but the play equipment, the layout, the park bench — everything was the same.

'We'll leave you to it but call me if you need me,' he said as the girls tugged him towards the swings.

Jennifer nodded and watched them go. Slowly, she looked at her surroundings, memories flashing before her eyes as she made her way over to the bench. When she looked down at the grass she could imagine

Arturo lying there, talking as he pointed to the clouds. A smile touched her lips at the vibrant way he'd always been able to make her feel. Her breathing became deeper as one emotion after another started to swamp her. The smile disappeared and a regretful sadness settled over her heart.

They would have had a great life together. She knew that without a doubt but it had been a life that wasn't meant to be. A life that didn't belong to her. Not any more.

She looked over at the play equipment, watching the children having so much fun, her eyes eagerly searching out a tall, dark and handsome man with two blonde cherubs beside him. When she found Jasper and the girls, Jennifer's breathing began to return to normal and to her surprise and delight, when she looked at him, she became filled with that same sense of vibrance she used to get from Arturo.

Her past was her past.

Jasper and the girls were her future.

He looked over at her then and she smiled and waved. Jasper settled the girls in the sandpit before striding towards her.

'OK?'

'Yes.' The word was soft but full of determination.

He didn't say anything else but came and

sat beside her, lacing his fingers through hers. They sat there for a while in silence, watching the girls playing happily together. Finally, it was Jennifer who broke the silence.

'I love your girls, Jasper.'

He smiled. 'They're pretty special. They have a way, through their innocence, to help us to breathe, to have fun, to laugh and enjoy life.' He shifted and placed his arm around her shoulders, bringing her closer. 'This world isn't done with you, Jennifer Thorngate. There's still so much you need to accomplish and whatever your goals are, whatever it is that you feel you need to do, I'll be right there beside you, supporting you every step of the way. And the girls will be there, too. My parents adore you, the girls can't stop talking about you, and I can't stop thinking about you, loving you.' He kissed her.

'Keep the memories,' he continued. 'No one wants to take them away from you but they're snapshots, Jen. Snapshots of another part of your life, another time, another place. We grow, we progress, we change. It's been happening since the moment of creation. You've grown, you've progressed and you've changed. Embrace it.'

Jennifer looked up at him with all of the

love in her heart. 'I intend to. Thank you for bringing me here, Jasper. Thank you for sharing your family with me, for being there for me and helping me through.' She held his gaze but swallowed, knowing she needed to continue, knowing she needed to tell him how she felt, even though she was apprehensive.

'Thank you for loving me.' Her voice was so choked with emotion that it dropped to a whisper. She swallowed, her heart pounding wildly against her ribs as she licked her lips. 'And because you love me, because of everything you and the girls have done . . . Jasper . . . I've fallen in love with you, too.'

'You have?' He'd known, he was sure he'd felt it, but there was always that tiny little part of him that doubted and now, that tiny little part had been swept away with her declaration.

'Yes.' She laughed through her emotion, relief mixed with passion flooding her as he gathered her close and pressed his mouth to hers. When he pulled away, he looked at her, unable to believe how incredibly happy he was. He looked over to where his girls were supposed to be playing in the sandpit but instead they were running towards them. He let go of Jennifer momentarily to scoop his daughters up, Lilly sitting on Jennifer's

knee and Lola on his own. He held his girls
— all three of them — in his arms but his
eyes were intent on Jennifer's.

'You'll marry me?'

Jennifer looked from Lola to Lilly and
then back to their daddy. 'Yes.'

'You going to marry our daddy?' Lola
asked, her eyes widening in surprise.

'You going to be our new mummy?' Lilly
asked, equally as surprised.

'Yes. Yes.' Jennifer laughed and kissed both
girls before kissing their father again.

'And you'll have a big wedding?' Lilly
asked.

'Yes,' Jasper answered.

'And in the church and have the party and
everything?' Lola was starting to wriggle
with delight.

'Yes. Everything.'

The girls looked at each other with glee.
'Finally,' they said in unison.

'Finally, what?' Jasper asked, a little
astonished at his daughters' perceptiveness.

'Finally we get to walk down the aisle!'
Both girls clapped their hands before running off to the slippery-slide, more than
happy to leave their father to kiss their new
mother once again.

The employees of Thorndike Press hope you have enjoyed this Large Print book. All our Thorndike, Wheeler, and Kennebec Large Print titles are designed for easy reading, and all our books are made to last. Other Thorndike Press Large Print books are available at your library, through selected bookstores, or directly from us.

For information about titles, please call:
  (800) 223-1244

or visit our Web site at:
  http://gale.cengage.com/thorndike

To share your comments, please write:
  Publisher
  Thorndike Press
  295 Kennedy Memorial Drive
  Waterville, ME 04901